His blue gaze zeroed in on her face. He had a way of looking at a person that seemed to see past any façade, to mak̶̶̶̶̶̶ ̶̶̶̶̶t hard to hide.

Like the fact th̶̶̶̶̶̶̶̶̶̶̶̶̶̶̶̶̶̶̶̶̶̶̶̶̶̶̶̶̶̶̶ ̶o his smile, his eyes, ̶̶̶̶̶̶̶̶̶̶̶̶̶̶̶̶̶̶̶̶̶̶̶̶̶̶̶̶̶̶̶ seen women get so w̶̶̶̶̶̶̶̶̶̶̶̶̶̶̶̶̶̶̶̶̶̶̶̶ ̶̶̶̶̶̶̶ ̶̶ime, that they tripped over̶̶̶̶̶̶̶̶̶̶̶̶̶̶̶ ̶wo feet trying to get closer to him. No wonder. Being this close to Caleb Lewis, she realized the direct power of his gaze. Almost…hypnotic.

Sarah cleared her throat. "Information? On what?"

"I wanted to ask whether you—" He cut the sentence off, then leaned forward. "What's that?"

"What's what?" She pivoted to follow his line of sight. Right over the books on her desk, past the coffee cup serving as a pencil holder, beyond the unopened oat-and-honey granola bar she'd been saving for a snack, and straight to—

The Wanted poster.

She reached to hide it, but Caleb's reach was faster and he plucked it up. "Hmm. Interesting."

"It's nothing." Sarah swiped at the paper, but Caleb just leaned away from her. "Give it back."

"'Missing: One shoe,'" he read. "'Red stiletto. Custom design. Reward for safe return.'" He arched a brow. "You lost a shoe?"

Dear Reader,

Anyone who knows me knows I love shoes. My closet is filled to the brim with stilettos, peep-toe pumps, slingbacks, boots—you name it, if it's cute (and especially if it's on sale), it's probably on my closet shelves. I can't pass the shoe department without at least stopping in and seeing what's new.

Need a clue that you're in the shoe department way too often? If the salesman remembers your name *and* your shoe size. I'm thinking of inviting the shoe sales staff to my next family barbecue. I think I'm personally putting a few of their kids through college.

So when I was asked to write a book for the In Her Shoes… miniseries, I was thrilled. It took a little brainstorming, but eventually the idea that is now *If the Red Slipper Fits…* came together. For me, the idea boiled down to one basic element—what's the worst that could happen to a pair of really cool shoes?

If you've read *The Other Wife,* then you know this isn't my first book where shoes make a starring appearance! I hope you enjoy *If the Red Slipper Fits….* I know I had a great time writing it! Sarah and Caleb were fabulous characters to work with, and their story became about so much more than a pair of shoes. Shoes that I found myself wishing were real, because they'd sure make a great addition to my collection!

I love to hear from readers, so feel free to visit my Web site at www.shirleyjump.com, try my recipes on my blog, www.shirleyjump.blogspot.com, or write to me at P.O. Box 5126, Fort Wayne, IN 46895. Happy reading and happy shoe shopping!

Shirley

SHIRLEY JUMP

If the Red Slipper Fits...

In Her Shoes

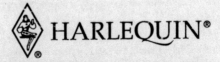

HARLEQUIN®

TORONTO • NEW YORK • LONDON
AMSTERDAM • PARIS • SYDNEY • HAMBURG
STOCKHOLM • ATHENS • TOKYO • MILAN • MADRID
PRAGUE • WARSAW • BUDAPEST • AUCKLAND

If you purchased this book without a cover you should be aware that this book is stolen property. It was reported as "unsold and destroyed" to the publisher, and neither the author nor the publisher has received any payment for this "stripped book."

Recycling programs
for this product may
not exist in your area.

ISBN-13: 978-0-373-74059-8

IF THE RED SLIPPER FITS...

First North American Publication 2010

Copyright © 2010 by Shirley Kawa-Jump, LLC

All rights reserved. Except for use in any review, the reproduction or utilization of this work in whole or in part in any form by any electronic, mechanical or other means, now known or hereafter invented, including xerography, photocopying and recording, or in any information storage or retrieval system, is forbidden without the written permission of the publisher, Harlequin Enterprises Limited, 225 Duncan Mill Road, Don Mills, Ontario, Canada M3B 3K9.

This is a work of fiction. Names, characters, places and incidents are either the product of the author's imagination or are used fictitiously, and any resemblance to actual persons, living or dead, business establishments, events or locales is entirely coincidental.

This edition published by arrangement with Harlequin Books S.A.

For questions and comments about the quality of this book please contact us at Customer_eCare@Harlequin.ca.

® and TM are trademarks of the publisher. Trademarks indicated with ® are registered in the United States Patent and Trademark Office, the Canadian Trade Marks Office and in other countries.

www.eHarlequin.com

Printed in U.S.A.

New York Times bestselling author **Shirley Jump** didn't have the willpower to diet, nor the talent to master under-eye concealer, so she bowed out of a career in television and opted instead for a career where she could be paid to eat at her desk—writing. At first, seeking revenge on her children for their grocery-store tantrums, she sold embarrassing essays about them to anthologies. However, it wasn't enough to feed her growing addiction to writing funny. So she turned to the world of romance novels, where messes are (usually) cleaned up before The End. In the worlds Shirley gets to create and control, the children listen to their parents, the husbands always remember holidays and the housework is magically done by elves. Though she's thrilled to see her books in stores around the world, Shirley mostly writes because it gives her an excuse to avoid cleaning the toilets and helps feed her shoe habit. To learn more, visit her Web site at www.shirleyjump.com.

Praise for Shirley Jump

"Shirley Jump's *Miracle on Christmas Eve* has a solid plot and involving conflict, and the characters are wonderful."
—*RT Book Reviews*

About *Sweetheart Lost and Found*
"This tale of rekindled love is right on target;
a delightful start to this uplifting, marriage-oriented series
[The Wedding Planners]."
—*Library Journal*

About *New York Times* bestselling anthology *Sugar and Spice*
"Jump's office romance gives the collection a kick,
with fiery writing."
—*Publishers Weekly*

To Marci, for being the best walking buddy and friend anyone could ask for. Rain or shine, you're there, to commiserate, cry, laugh (and yes, sometimes, shop). Thank you.

CHAPTER ONE

SARAH Griffin watched the red shoe wing past her, then tumble in slow, horrible motion, toe over heel, out the open window and into oblivion. Shock kept her rooted to the floor for a good half second, before the horror of what had just happened pricked her like a pair of spurs, and she dived, too late, for the custom-designed, one-of-a-kind Frederick K red stiletto.

The shoe that was going to make or break her career—the same shoe that had just made a three-story disappearing act.

"How could you do that?" The words exploded from her throat, but elicited no response from her younger sister, standing just a few feet from the window. "Don't you know how important that shoe is?" Sarah leaned out the window, searching for the burst of crimson leather on the gray concrete. Nothing, nothing, then—

There. By a trash can. Relief surged in her chest. Okay, the shoe was still intact. Seemed okay, at least from here, but she'd never know for sure until she retrieved it. She wheeled away from the window and dashed for the door.

"Where are you going?" Honest surprise lit the notes in her sister's voice. Sarah paused and gaped at Diana. Did she really expect her to stay here and finish the argument?

Diana Griffin had a slender frame, but it covered for a surprisingly strong body. She spent her afternoons beating up a punching bag at Gold's Gym, so much that they'd replaced it twice in the two years Diana had been a member.

You didn't mess with Diana. Sarah knew that, and hadn't heeded her own advice. Match Diana's temper with Sarah's tendency to blurt out her true feelings, and you ended up with a disaster. Now the shoe—*the shoe*—was on the sidewalk and her career was hanging by an ever-unraveling thread.

"I have to get that shoe back," Sarah said. "Do you know what's going to happen if—"

"Let it go, Sarah." Diana waved in dismissal. *No biggie,* she was saying. Diana had made her point, using her right pitching arm, and Sarah should just *get over it already.* "It's just a shoe. If you want something cute and pretty, I'll give you a pair of mine."

Sarah threw up her hands and shoved past Diana. "You don't get it, Diana. You never do."

Her sister shook her head. "Get what? That you are trying to ruin my life…again?"

Drama. There was always drama with her younger sister. It was as if Diana hadn't gotten enough attention as a kid and was in a constant quest for more. Hence the hyperbole and the temper-tantrum shoe fling. Sarah had seen more than one model diva pull the same stunt, and over the most ridiculously unimportant things, like a corner table or a too-warm glass of chardonnay. It was the kind of behavior that filled the gossip pages at *Behind the Scenes*. Written by Sarah herself.

She was tired of the drama, the look-at-me antics of the people she covered for the tabloid. Just once, she'd like to see someone defy the stereotypes she blurbed with oversized headlines. Someone who got honest, admitted that the club scene was as shallow as a puddle, and that there were more important things in life than starring on page six.

"I don't have time for this, Diana." Sarah opened the door, hurried down the hall, bypassing the elevator for the stairs and then burst out the front door of her apartment building and onto the congested street of her Manhattan neighborhood. Traffic hummed, garbage trucks bleated and construction crews hammered, creating the morning melodies of the city. She had loved this neighborhood the second she stepped foot in it, finding a small apartment in an old brownstone and a kindly landlord who brought her cookies on Christmas Eve.

Her apartment was insanely small, and yes, a third-floor walk-up without any of the fanciness of a doorman or an elevator. But the neighborhood had charm and a genuine quality about it that Sarah craved at the end of the day.

The bright fall sun blinded Sarah for a second, bouncing off her glasses and giving her twin bursts of yellow in her vision. She pivoted to the right, toward Mrs. Sampson's trash cans, fully expecting to see the shoe right there. Just where she'd seen it a few seconds ago.

The space by the landlord's trashcan was empty. Well, not empty—a crumpled soda can, two ketchup-spattered fast-food burger wrappers and a torn Chinese-food box leaking its leftovers in a dark puddle—but empty of the most important thing in Sarah Griffin's life right now.

The shoe.

Panic fluttered in her chest. It couldn't be gone. *Couldn't be.* It wasn't like it could walk off, right? And who would only want one shoe? What would be the value in a solo stiletto?

And that shoe, of all the ones in the world. Completely impractical, good only for special occasions. Surely, no one would take it?

If the shoe wasn't here, though, that meant someone had it. The question was who? And why?

She glanced around, looking for someone carrying a red high heel. Hurried businesspeople crowded the sidewalk, all of them so intent on getting to their skyscraper destinations, they powered right past her in their sneakers and loafers. Not a one held a shoe.

A tall dark-haired man in a navy pinstriped suit had stopped a few yards away from her. From this distance and angle, she couldn't tell if she knew him or not. Heck, most of the men on the street looked the same from the back—all suit and dress shoes. She saw him shrug, reach into his jacket, then continue on his way. Could he have the shoe?

She watched him for a moment longer, then decided no. From behind, he looked too much like the guy next door—albeit, the handsome guy next door—to be the kind that would pick up a stray shoe and walk away with it. She considered running after him, just in case, but then he hailed an oncoming cab and was gone before she could get her feet to coordinate with her brain. Damn.

The shoe had to be here. Somewhere. Sarah bent down and drew closer to the trash cans. Maybe a rat had dragged it into the dark corners? The thought made her sick, but she looked anyway. She looked behind, in front of, beside and even under the dark brown plastic containers.

No footwear of any kind.

Now the panic was clawing at her throat, threatening to cut off her air supply. This was not happening. So, so, so not happening. Karl was going to kill her. No, not just kill her—maim her, behead her and then hang her decapitated body in the parking lot as an example of idiocy.

How on earth was she ever going to get off the gossip pages of the tabloid and move over to and into the main section of *Smart Fashion* magazine if she couldn't keep hold of a simple shoe? It wasn't just the Frederick K that had gone sailing out the window—it was every dream she'd had for her career.

For months, she'd wanted to switch to the editorial staff of *Smart Fashion,* the monthly magazine put out by the same parent company that did the tabloid. One magazine was the shining respected industry publication; the other was the back-stabbing stepsister. At the time, working for the tabloid had been a job, one that paid well. One she'd needed desperately. She'd seen it as a stepping stone, a temporary stop.

It had become a long-term stall. One she hated

more and more every day. Moving to *Smart Fashion* and covering the newest trends in jewelry and skirt lengths didn't exactly call for deep journalistic investigation, but it was a step in the right direction. A step away from the years she'd spent observing and penning exclamation-point-studded stories about how the "glamorous" people lived.

She was tired of working in the shadows. Tired of putting her future on hold. This shoe, as silly as it sounded, had been the symbol of everything Sarah intended to change about her job, herself and most of all, her life.

Fifteen minutes of frantic searching passed before Sarah was forced to admit the shoe was gone. She ran back up to her apartment, and headed straight for the window, ignoring Diana sitting on the sofa, filing her nails with the kind of calm that said she had no idea what kind of damage she'd just done. Or if she did, she didn't care—

Both were typical Diana.

Sarah and her sister shared a lot in the genes department—they were both slender, both had long, dark brown hair with a touch of red that turned to gold after too much time in the sun, and both had wide green eyes. But when it came to sensitivity and empathy, there were many days when Sarah wondered what had happened to her sister's. She loved Diana, but her inability to relate to other people's problems chafed at their relationship like a splinter. It was as if Diana had decided Sarah did enough worrying and caring for the both of them.

"Please let it be there," Sarah whispered. She leaned forward, out the window, scanning the sidewalk a second time.

Nothing. The shoe was gone.

Sarah sank to the oak floor of her apartment. "I'm so dead."

"I don't know why you're making such a big deal out of this," Diana said, flinging out her fingers to check her emery job. "It's just a shoe."

"It's my *job*." And so much more, Sarah thought, but didn't say. Her sister would never understand what that shoe represented. How it was so much more than her first big project for *Smart Fashion* magazine. Okay, so not exactly big—just a quarter-page write-up on the launch of the line by Frederick K, with a review of the premier stiletto in the collection. But it was a start, and that was all Sarah needed.

She couldn't make Diana see how that simple strappy red heel seemed to hold everything Sarah had always wanted—and had thus far denied herself. "Not just that, but that shoe is a one-of-a-kind, secret prototype that no one was supposed to see before the spring fashion shows. No one."

Diana shrugged. "You did."

"You're not helping the situation, Diana."

"I'll buy you another pair. There. Problem solved."

"You *can't* buy these. That's the point. No one is supposed to have them until after the spring fashion shows. My boss trusted me to keep them under wraps, and now—"

What was she going to do? How on earth was she going to explain this? The photo shoot for the fall issue was only three days away, and half of the starring product had disappeared. The magazine had everything laid out and ready to go, with space left for photos and stories from coverage of Fashion Week in two weeks. The top designers would be showcasing their spring fashions for next year, and all of New York would be abuzz with chatter about their new designs. It was the biggest week of the year at the magazine, one where tensions ran high and expectations ran higher.

She couldn't make Diana see that, nor, Sarah was sure, could she get her sister to understand why she had taken the stilettos home in the first place. Explaining to Karl the little field trip she'd taken those designer shoes on was going to be even harder than telling him she'd lost one half of the pair.

Why did you take those one-of-a-kind Frederick Ks home, Sarah?

Because I thought having them, just for a little while, would transform my life.

Oh, yeah, that was going to go over well. Like, unemployment-line well.

"Well, we have a problem. And we need to deal with it right away." Diana tucked the emery board away, then flipped out a lipstick case and slicked on a crimson bow.

"That's the understatement of the year. You just singlehandedly sent my career down the fast track to nowhere. Gee, thanks, Diana."

"I didn't mean with that silly shoe." Diana sighed, then met her sister's gaze. "I meant with Dad. You are not dumping him at my apartment. I have a life, you know."

They were back to this again? Sarah shouldn't be surprised. Diana was the kind to pick at an issue until she got the answer she wanted. Preferably one that absolved her of all responsibility.

For years, Sarah had taken on the caretaker role. When their mother had first gotten sick, it had been Sarah who stepped in to be the lady of the house. Heartbreak over his wife's cancer had immobilized their father, leaving Sarah two choices—let everything go to hell, or step into her mother's apron.

Bridget Griffin had lingered, in that limbo between life and death, for almost ten years before death finally ended her suffering. For so many years, Sarah had expected the death, but when that day finally came—

She'd found herself standing there, stunned. A hole had opened up in her life, and she had yet to find a way to fill it. *Live your life,* her father had said.

What life? she'd wanted to say back. For so many years, she'd poured everything into her family. No time for dating, for daydreaming or for thinking about the paths she might have taken, if only...

All those *if onlys* had been lived by Diana. Sarah had made sure her little sister got to experience everything—dates, proms, parties— even if that meant Sarah was the one waiting up at home instead of doing the same thing. Or working insane hours to help pay for Diana's dreams.

Their father had worked hard all his life, but a cop's salary only went so far. As his wife's illness worsened, he became less attentive to the holes in the family budget, so Sarah went to work, adding what she could to the family coffers. Never telling her father, just quietly taking care of them all.

Which meant her life had been put on hold for so long, she'd forgotten what it meant to have one outside of work. Working a job that paid well but that grated on her conscience on a daily basis. Sarah Griffin needed a change—and she'd thought that bringing home the Frederick Ks would be the first step.

Kinda hard to take any step at all only wearing one shoe.

"Diana, you promised," Sarah said, returning her attention to the problem at hand—what to do about Dad. "You can't just back out on that because it's inconvenient."

Her sister winced. The truth had hit its mark. "I can't drop everything just because you've decided that Dad has overstayed his welcome. I mean, I have a job, friends—"

"And what, I don't?" Sarah said.

Diana bit off a laugh. "Sarah, I don't want to be mean, but seriously, you have all the social life of wallpaper. I'm out every night. I can't be babysitting Dad."

"I'm out, too. More nights than I'd like to be."

"Yeah, writing about how *other* people are living their lives. That doesn't make you a social butterfly."

Sarah brushed off her sister's words. The magazine paid her to cover those events. So what if doing so left her little time to do anything more than watch and write? She was the one who was being responsible. Doing her duty as a daughter, letting her father stay with her for the last few weeks. "I'm doing my job, sis. Something I'd be able to focus on more if you stuck to your promise. Dad won't be staying long with you."

Okay, so Sarah couldn't really promise that. Martin Griffin had already been in her apartment—him and his godawful ugly recliner—for over a year. After their mother had died, Martin had wandered around the empty, quiet family home for several months before Sarah finally convinced him to put it on the market. He wasn't good at living on his own—he had spent far too many years on the police force and was more used to male camaraderie than to running a house. He forgot to eat dinner, forgot to transfer the wet clothes to the dryer, forgot to put the basket in the coffeepot. Sarah had stopped by twice a day, worried he'd hurt himself one of these days, and finally she'd just suggested he move in with her. Her father, for all his grumpiness, seemed to enjoy living at Sarah's, and tried to help out in his own way. Not necessarily the way Sarah wanted, but she loved her father and had enjoyed him living with her.

Still, she wanted her independence. The freedom from worrying. She'd worried for years—about the house, about her father, about her sister and mostly about her mother—and the responsibilities weighed so heavily on her shoulders, she was surprised she wasn't stooped over. It was Diana's turn to be the responsible one. To take some of the burden from Sarah.

Except Diana didn't want any responsibility and never had. Maybe Sarah had made a mistake in being so indulgent with her little sister.

The lipstick went back in her sister's purse, replaced by a travel hairbrush and a hand mirror. "I'm in the middle of planning the Horticultural Society Charity Ball. It's my first big job out of college, and it's super important, Sarah. I don't have time for this...distraction."

Sarah didn't mention that the "job" her sister spoke of was a volunteer position, given to her by her boyfriend's mother, who chaired the Horticultural Society. Her sister had yet to find employment she could stick with longer than a few weeks.

"That distraction is your father." Sarah shook her head. "I swear, we are not related."

"Let him stay here. He likes you better anyway."

Sarah glanced over at her sister, but Diana

was immersed in sweeping her bangs into a soft C shape. "Diana, he loves us both equally."

Diana snorted. "I have two dogs, Sarah. And I definitely like one better than the other."

"We're his children, not his pets. Family ties run much deeper than flea collars."

Diana arched a brow. "But, Sarah," and now her voice dropped into a whine, "you're good at dealing with Dad. I don't even get along with him."

"What better way to build a relationship than by having him move in?" Sarah gave her sister a smile. A firm smile.

"I'd rather buy him tickets to the next Mets game."

"Sorry, sis, but it's your turn." Sarah crossed her arms over her chest. "You might have trashed my career today, but I'm not letting you get out of this, too. At the end of this month we'll get him moved over." They'd had this same argument just thirty minutes ago—and look where it had ended up. With Diana picking up the thing closest to her and pitching it out the window.

Sarah refused to budge this time. For too long, she'd acquiesced at the cost of her own plans. The day she'd walked out of the office with the Frederick Ks impulsively shoved into her tote bag had been the day she'd decided she would stop being the responsible, dependable one. If she didn't put her foot down now and demand that those around her change, then things might never move past where they'd been, and that wasn't an option.

Except now she was too worried about finding that damned shoe to do anything *but* be responsible.

Diana sputtered out one last protest. "But—"

"No. It's settled. I'm not having this discussion anymore. If I ever find that shoe—" And Sarah was beginning to despair of ever seeing it again, but she couldn't think of that right now or she would go insane. "—I'll be working nonstop at the magazine. This is my big break. Dad hates to be left alone, and you know how he gets if no one is here to be with him."

"I can't. I have—"

Sarah crossed to her sister. The sight of the shoe spiraling out the window came back to her mind, along with years of frustration. She met Diana's gaze and held her ground. "You have family who needs you, Diana. That's all there is to it."

"You're wrong about that," Diana said, her voice low and quiet.

Was everything okay with Diana? The familiar worry, which she had felt for so many years, during which she'd been as much mother to Diana as sister, sprang to life in Sarah. Her confident, beautiful little sister rarely betrayed vulnerability or weakness. She had always been, as people said, a "handful," a spitfire. And yet, a sense of melancholy seemed to be painted on Diana's features. "Diana, are you all right?"

Sarah reached for her sister, but Diana rose, tucked the brush and mirror back into her purse, then headed for the door. "If Dad moved in with me, it would be a disaster. Please, Sarah. Let him stay with you. It'll be easier all around." For a second, Sarah considered relenting. To release Diana from a duty she didn't want. Then her sister said the words that made Sarah solidify her resolve. "Face it, Sarah. You're the one we all rely on. You're the only responsible one in the family."

"I don't want to be," Sarah said to her sister's retreating form as Diana left the apartment. "Not anymore."

Caleb Lewis propped the shoe on the top shelf of the credenza behind his desk, then sat back in his chair and stared at the slender red stiletto he'd found that morning. Size 7, sleek in all its crimson curves and sporting a racy T-strap design. The thing had literally dropped from the sky, practically into his hands. What were the chances?

It had to be a fake. Couldn't be the super-secret, big hush-hush prototype for Frederick K's much-anticipated shoe line. Ever since he'd opened his doors, women had been buying every dress, blouse and skirt that the hotshot rising Boston designer made. They'd stood in line for hours just for a chance to buy a cocktail dress. Nearly come to blows over the launch of his cashmere sweaters last fall.

Frederick K was the hot shiny new toy in the fashion industry, and LL Designs had been trying to play catch-up ever since. Caleb had taken over his mother's company a little more than a year ago, when LL Designs was at its height of popularity. And immediately after he'd seen Frederick K come on the scene and steal away their business, one design at a time, like a mouse nibbling at a piece of cheese.

In that time, the stakes had risen. Hit by a hard economy, a decrease in couture spending, and the additional competition, Caleb had been trying to resurrect the business for months. But he lacked his mother's eye for women's designs, and everything the rest of the designers had come up with lacked that LL Designs spark. Caleb couldn't say what was missing, only that the products just weren't the same.

Hell, nothing had been the same since he'd taken over for his mother, stepping into a position he had no business filling. At the time, the options had been almost nil. Lenora had been here one day, then fighting for her life the next. Without the company founder at the helm, the employees had gone into a panic. The only option was to fill the CEO position with someone who cared as much about the company as Lenora. It was supposed to be a temporary fix until he could afford to hire a CEO.

It hadn't been long before Caleb realized how much he cared about the company wasn't enough to offset his lack of experience. Nor did it help the company run effectively and profitably. He should have been smart and hired a new head designer, at the very least. But as the company funds dwindled, the dollars for any additional staff disappeared. At the time, Caleb had thought he could handle it.

After all, this was just dresses and blouses. How hard could it be?

Apparently plenty hard, and not at all the kind of thing a former marketing director could do. He knew all about how to sell the product to the consumer—the problem he had was creating a product consumers actually liked.

This spring's fashion shows were the make-or-break-it opportunity for LL Designs. Either get the public's attention this year or close the doors of the decades-old fashion house. And admit that he had singlehandedly run his mother's life's work into the ground. If she knew what had happened to her company…well, it was a blessing that she didn't.

Way to go, Caleb. Want to blow up a small village while you're at it?

"That isn't…" His assistant Martha Nessbaum stopped by his desk, and put a hand over her mouth. He hadn't even heard the older woman come in—that alone showed how distracted he'd become in the last few weeks. Caleb Lewis, who had always been on top of the smallest detail in his former career, was clearly losing his focus. "Is it?"

"Maybe," Caleb said. "It sure fits the leaked description."

"Can I touch it?"

"Martha, it's a shoe, not the Hope diamond."

Martha shot him a you-don't-get-it look. "This isn't just a shoe, Caleb, it's…sex on a heel."

Caleb chuckled. He hadn't expected his sixtyish, lion-at-the-door assistant to say that. "Women and shoes. Once researchers figure out how to cure cancer and how Stonehenge was built, I'm sure they'll get right to work on that mystery."

"How did you get hold of it?"

"Someone lost it."

"What do you mean someone *lost* it? Who

would do that?" Martha's gaze narrowed. "You didn't break into the Frederick K factory and steal it, did you?"

He laughed. "No. I'm not that desperate."

Yet. How long until he was? LL Designs employed four hundred people. Four hundred people who counted on him to pay their mortgages, send their kids to college, put food on their tables. It wasn't just the thought of destroying Lenora Lewis's legacy that ate him up at night—

It was the thought of all those people standing in the unemployment line. Because of him.

For the thousandth time he wondered what insanity had made him think he could handle running this company. Hell, he could barely handle his own life. He'd made enough mistakes to fill a cruise ship. Maybe if he had—

No, he wasn't going to think about that. Water under the bridge—water that still churned in his gut with regrets.

Martha reached out and picked up the slender crimson heel. She cradled it in her palm as gently as a newborn kitten, and, he swore, nearly breathed in the scent of the leather. "It's beautiful. Absolutely—" She gasped, then turned the right side toward him and pointed at a slight scuff mark. "Oh, my God. What happened here?"

"An unfortunate meeting with concrete." The damage looked as if it could be buffed out, but either way, it didn't matter to Caleb. He wasn't photographing the shoe, or selling it or wearing it. Just using it for his own purposes.

The idea had come to him almost from the minute he picked up the Frederick K stiletto this morning. He'd been in such a rush to get to the meeting with the venue he was using for Fashion Week that he'd nearly missed the discarded high heel. But the flash of red drew his eye, and he found himself stopping, partly out of curiosity, partly out of some weird sixth sense that told him the forgotten shoe wasn't some Goodwill cast-off, but rather something big.

Very big.

Before he even picked it up, he recognized the trademark black striped underside that marked every Frederick K design. Then the scribbled autograph of the designer, sewn into the leather base. An *F,* a squiggle, then a *K*. The man could have been a doctor, given the disaster he made out of his own signature.

Before he could think about what he was doing, Caleb had tucked the shoe into his jacket, called a cab and headed to his meeting. Someone was undoubtedly missing this shoe—

But Caleb sure as hell wasn't missing this opportunity to one-up the shark threatening to send LL Designs to the bottom of the crowded, competitive fashion ocean. People were counting on him to keep this ship afloat, and by God, he'd do that.

Yeah, but how? the little voice in the back of his head asked. He couldn't let his employees down. But most of all, couldn't let his mother down. She might not be aware of what was happening with the company, but he held on to the thought that maybe someday she would be back, and if she returned, she'd want to see that he had been a good steward of her legacy.

"So...now that you have the elusive Frederick K shoe," Martha said, "what are you going to do with it?" She clutched it to her chest, as if she couldn't part with the right-foot treasure.

Caleb leaned forward and pried the stiletto out of Martha's hand, then put it back on his shelf. "Keep it. And then rush an even hotter design into production. We've been talking about launching a line of shoes for years, and we got all geared up to do just that before the bottom dropped out of the industry. I think now's the time. This just fell into my lap—literally—and it'd be insane not to take advantage of it."

"You're finally going to take that leap?" Martha's smile widened in approval. "It's about damned time."

He chuckled. "Yeah. It probably is."

"And for what it's worth, your mother would be proud."

The words sent a sharp pang through Caleb. Proud. Would she be?

Caleb's gaze landed on the painting of his mother that hung on the far wall. The oil likeness had captured a younger Lenora, not the woman he knew now. A constant smile curved across her face, and her platinum-blond hair was piled on top of her head in a loose chignon, the same one she'd worn nearly every day, half the time with a pencil stuck in the knot. She seemed to be looking down on him and patiently waiting for him to pull off a miracle.

To do the right thing.

He closed his eyes, unable to look at her image another second. The right thing. Did he even know what that was?

"Proud?" Caleb said, looking away from his mother's image. "Of what I've done to her company? Of how I've nearly ruined a lifetime of work in a little over a year?"

Martha leaned in toward him, her expression stern. "You got on the back of a wild elephant when you took the reins of this company. I know it's been difficult, but you're doing a better job than you think. And now..." She pressed a hand to her chest and the smile returned. "...you're taking a risk. Jumping off into the

great unknown. That's the kind of thing
Lenora did."

He hadn't thought about launching a shoe line
as repeating his mother's brazen business antics.
If that was so, then maybe this was the ticket
to relaunching the company into a successful
orbit.

"What are you going to use for designs?"
Martha asked.

He toyed with the heel of the shoe. It was truly
a work of art, all sleek lines, with a deep V at
the toe and a T-strap edged in gold metallic. "I
was thinking of letting Kenny try his hand at a
couple—"

"Don't. He doesn't get shoes. I should know,
I'm a girl." Martha smiled. "An old girl, but one
who still loves her shoes."

Martha had a point. The problem was, talented designers weren't exactly in great supply at
LL Designs. Just before his mother stepped
down, the company had lost two of the best
on staff, then another two as the economy had
dragged the once-profitable company down.
And the inspiration for the company, the one
with all the ideas, was too ill for consultation.
Maybe forever.

Somehow, Caleb had to do this on his own,
and do it better than he had been doing for the
past year. "Maybe I'll have to hire some outside

help," he said, though he still didn't know how he could afford that. Caleb rose, scooping up the shoe and his BlackBerry. "Either way, I'll figure it out." The weight of every decision he made hung heavy on his shoulders. Was this shoe—and the company's entry into footwear—the miracle he needed? Maybe. Though a whisper of doubt told him if he didn't fix the problems he was having with the collection as a whole, footwear wasn't going to resurrect LL Designs, either. "I'm going to pop over to *Smart Fashion* and see if I can get any buzz on the Frederick K collection."

And maybe see if he could find out why this shoe had been on the ground. There were very few people in the industry who would have access to this accessory. The magazine, which had been a favorite of Frederick K's for years, was at the top of his mental list. Someone there had to know something about this shoe, and maybe even what the designer had in store for the rest of his shoe line.

"You're going yourself?" Martha asked.

Caleb nodded.

"But you hate the media. *Especially* that magazine."

The headlines flashed in his head again. The question marks, the massive black letters, all of them trying to capitalize on his mother's sudden retirement, and then return like vultures to pick at every misstep the company had made since then. Not just the company, but his own life, too. He'd become the punching bag of the gossip column at *Behind the Scenes,* the tabloid arm of *Smart Fashion.* Every move he made was chronicled in living color. Yes, he hated the media, and hated *Behind the Scenes* the most. The tabloid was nothing but trash with advertising.

The problem—it and its sister publication were the highest-circulation trash with advertising in his industry.

Either way, he didn't trust the media. He'd learned early on that those in the media wanted only one thing—the headline, no matter the personal carnage along the way.

"You haven't exactly been Mr. Friendly with the reporters in the past." Martha made a face. "They're still talking about that incident in Milan."

And still making him pay for it, too, with one gossip-riddled story after another. The reporters had focused their laser eyes on his love life—or what they surmised about his love life—rather than the company. It had netted him nothing but bad press. Press he could hardly afford, given the shaky state of LL Designs lately.

If he was smart, he'd stay home every night. Staying home meant allowing the quiet to get to him, letting his thoughts travel down the very paths he was using the lights and noises of night-clubs to help him avoid.

At least the tabloids hadn't uncovered the one truth that would put the final nail in the coffin of his reputation. So far, the reporters had been content to focus on his nightlife rather than where he spent every Tuesday, Thursday and Saturday afternoon. He'd taken great pains to assure his mother's privacy was maintained. An out-of-state rehab facility. A well-paid, compassionate nursing team. And a constant request for discretion from all who knew Lenora.

"Maybe if you were nice to those reporters," Martha said, interrupting his thoughts, "you'd get better results."

Caleb scowled. "Nice? To the media?" His mother would lecture him to no end if he became overly friendly with reporters.

"Those flies perk up and listen when you ply them with honey."

"Yeah, then they turn around and breed a bunch of maggots all over my still-breathing body."

Martha wagged a finger at him. "Maybe you're the one that needs the honey."

"All right." He let out a sigh. "I'll bring the editorial staff some cookies or something."

Martha laughed. "For a man who heads a

fashion design house, you really are clueless about women. Shoes and chocolate, Caleb. That's all you need to get a woman's attention."

"And all this time I thought it was a rapier wit."

"Keep telling yourself that, funny man." Martha shot him a smile before she headed out of his office. "And see how far it gets you when there's a sale on Jimmy Choos."

CHAPTER TWO

As MUCH as she wanted to, Sarah couldn't hide out in her apartment and pray for a bunch of elves to knock on her door and hand over a replacement shoe. No, she had to be proactive.

Find that damned shoe, and at the same time, avoid Karl in the office. For a woman who had set out to change her life this week, she was certainly heading in the wrong direction.

Pedro Esposito leaned his dyed blond head over her cubicle wall. When she'd first arrived this morning, she'd dumped the entire sad story on the other writer's shoulder. Pedro was a good friend—the kind who wouldn't run to the boss and report Sarah's shoe loss just so he could get promoted over her. His listening ear and shoulder to cry on should have been marketed to every woman needing a trustable friend. "Good news, peach."

"There's good news today?"

Pedro nodded. "Don't you read your e-mails?

Karl had to have an emergency root canal, so he'll be out all day. Ding-dong, the boss is gone."

Sarah laughed. Relief burst inside her chest. She'd just been handed a twenty-four-hour reprieve. "Thank God."

"No, thank the walnut muffin that cracked his crown." Pedro grinned, then fluttered a piece of paper onto her desk. "Here. This should help save your job."

Sarah picked up the color flyer. "Oh, very funny, Pedro. A wanted poster for a missing shoe."

His smile widened. "Better than a wanted poster for your head on a stick, which is what Karl's going to hang up if he finds out what happened to that Frederick K."

Sarah shuddered. Knowing Karl, that was a distinct possibility. He had a tendency to freak out over everything from a missed deadline to a drop in advertising revenues. "I'll find it."

"Whatever you want to believe, Cinderella. But if you ask me, what you need is a prince to come along and save you." Pedro chuckled, then sank back behind his own desk.

No way. She was going to save herself, thank you very much. Hadn't she done a thousand stories on cheating, no-good men? On the kind of men who might pretend to be Prince Charming, but were really Prince Self-Serving in nice clothes? Men who went after the nearest pretty young thing, ignoring the steadfast quiet, not-so-glamorous girl in the corner.

She didn't need that. At all.

"This Cinderella is going to find her own shoe," Sarah said. "I made this mess. I'll figure out how to solve it. No fairy godmothers or princes necessary."

Sarah put the flyer on her desk. Maybe she'd duck out early, and knock on a few doors in her neighborhood. Someone had to have seen something. They *had* to have.

She got up, about to head over to the break room for more coffee, hoping to quell the headache that had started yesterday and had yet to subside, when she saw the last man she expected to see striding down the aisle.

Caleb Lewis.

Lord, he was good-looking. Too bad she knew what a cad he could be in real life. Nevertheless, the dark-haired owner of LL Designs had a way of carrying himself that demanded attention and drew her gaze to him, even against her better judgment. Lean and muscular, he stood several inches taller than her, just tall enough for a woman to curl against him and press her head to his chest, feel his heart beat and the solid strength of him. His blue eyes always seemed to hold a hint of a tease, as if he was ready to laugh at the slightest provocation. The kind of man who embodied fun. A good time.

The problem? He was known for exactly that—having a good time, and doing so in public. She'd watched from the sidelines dozens of times while Caleb Lewis laughed it up with the model of the week. Or tangoed on the dance floor in the middle of a sea of women. Or closed down the club, leaving with a woman on each arm. His nickname in the magazine was Devil-May-Care Caleb—a moniker Karl had come up with to describe the designer-house president's footloose attitude and lifestyle.

He was heart-stoppingly gorgeous—she'd give him that. Still, a handsome man who starred on the pages of the gossip column way too often. Apparently every woman in New York knew how gorgeous he was, and from what she'd observed, he'd spent every night appreciating that attention. Way too much.

Ever since she'd started writing about his active and highly social personal life, there'd been a war of sorts brewing between herself and LL Designs. One where he avoided her and she hounded him for the truth. Thus far, his favorite and only response was "No comment."

So what was he doing here?

He strode down the carpeted path between

the cubicles, then came to a stop. Right in front of her.

It had finally come to a head. He was here to confront her about the articles that had covered his endless squiring of one model after another. His wild antics in bars up and down the east coast. The reputation he'd garnered for being not just a ladies' man, but one who did what he wanted. When he wanted. Consequences be damned.

"Miss Griffin." Caleb Lewis nodded, his expression as unreadable as white walls.

Oh, God, he was here to sue her. That was the last thing she needed today. Then she noticed the oversized white wicker basket in his hands, a cellophane-wrapped treasure trove of chocolate goodies from the candy shop down the street.

What on earth?

"Can I help you with anything?" Sarah asked. "Do you need directions to Karl's office?" She gestured down the hall, to the staircase that led to the senior editor's office.

"Actually," he held up the basket, stuffed to the brim with brightly colored candies, thick, decadent chocolate bars and luscious cocoa mix packets. "I came to...bribe you."

Bribe her? After all she'd written about him? It had to be a trick. She snorted. "Yeah, right.

With what? Laxative-laced chocolates? Or did you put razor blades in the candied apples?"

A slight grin crossed his face. "I considered it."

"Honesty." Despite herself, she grinned back. "I can appreciate that."

Her stomach rumbled, and saliva pooled in her mouth. That basket held a minimum of three pounds of chocolate, she estimated. After the last twenty-odd hours, she could use at least a pound of the sugar solace in Caleb Lewis's hands.

He placed the basket on her desk, close enough that she could swipe one of those candy bars with little more than a scissor snip of the cellophane. She fought the urge. Valiantly.

Caleb gestured toward the visitor chair. She nodded, and he dropped into the seat with the kind of ease that marked a confident man, one who could take over a space simply by being in it. "I need some information."

Sarah tried to concentrate on Caleb's face instead of the candy. Her stomach rumbled in protest. She should have had breakfast this morning. Then again, concentrating on Caleb Lewis came with as many dangers as digesting the thousands of calories in the basket before her. The man was a distracting interruption she definitely didn't need today.

His blue gaze zeroed in on her face. He had a way of looking at a person that seemed to see past any façade, to make any secret hard to hide. Like the fact that her entire body was responding to his smile, his eyes, betraying her common sense. She'd seen women get so wrapped up in his face, his smile, that they tripped over their own two feet trying to get closer to him. No wonder. Being this close to Caleb Lewis, she realized the direct power of his gaze. Almost hypnotic.

Sarah cleared her throat. "Information? On what?"

"I wanted to ask whether you—" He cut the sentence off, then leaned forward. "What's that?"

"What's what?" She pivoted to follow his line of sight. Right over the books on her desk, past the coffee cup serving as a pencil holder, beyond the unopened oat-and-honey granola bar she'd been saving for a snack, and straight to—

The wanted poster.

She reached to hide it, but Caleb's reach was faster and he plucked it up. "Hmm. Interesting."

"It's nothing." Sarah swiped at the paper, but Caleb just leaned away from her. "Give it back."

"Missing: one shoe," he read. "Red stiletto.

Custom design. Reward for safe return." He arched a brow. "You lost a shoe?"

Sarah snatched the paper out of his hand and buried it under a stack of old magazine issues on her desk. In the next cubicle, she heard Pedro snicker. "I thought you wanted to talk about your company."

He leaned back in the chair, crossing his arms over his chest. "That looks like a Frederick K. I heard rumors he was launching a shoe line. Is this a prototype for the new season? Something he plans to unveil at Fashion Week?"

Suspicion arced inside her, then she realized the designer's trademark signature was clearly visible in the photo Pedro had used, one he'd probably grabbed off the server from the art department's test shoot last week. Someone like Caleb, who made his living in this industry, would recognize the logo right away, and would want information about the competition. "Maybe."

"Did you lose it?"

His stare seemed to cut right through her. But she refused to be daunted by him. Or by the condemnation in his tone. "What do you care?"

"Oh, I don't." A smile curved across his face. "Though *you* might, if you want to find that shoe."

The suspicion that had risen in her earlier

burst into full-bore distrust. For the first time, she realized he was wearing a navy-blue pin-striped suit. Just like the man she'd seen stop on the sidewalk this morning. Had he been that man? Had he found and taken the stiletto?

What were the chances? And surely, he would have told her right away, wouldn't he? Then again, given their history, the chances were slim he'd tell her anything. There were a lot of navy-blue-suit-wearing men out there.

But not very many interested in a Frederick K stiletto.

"What do you mean, *if* I want to find that shoe?" she asked.

He danced his fingers on the arm of his chair, that damnable grin lighting up his features. It was the kind of smile that said *I know something you don't.* "I might know where it is."

Relief exploded inside her, quickly chased by the sobering reality that this was *Caleb Lewis* she was talking to. The man hated her guts. His vague comments about the shoe's whereabouts could all be a trick. A way to get back at her for all those columns. "You have to return the shoe. It's private property."

That smile flitted across his face again, too fast to read its meaning. The tempting aroma of chocolate wafted up from the basket to greet

Sarah, as if saying, *trust him. He's okay. He came with chocolate.*

"Is there a reward involved?" Caleb asked.

"Mr. Lewis, if you have that shoe—"

"Maybe I do. Maybe I don't. Either way, I'm not admitting anything, because Lord knows you're very good at declaring me guilty before you've looked at all the facts." He draped an arm over the back of the chair, as easy with being there as if he were in his own office. "Why don't you meet me over at my office at say, two o'clock, and we can discuss an…arrangement of sorts."

One more smile—the same smile that had undoubtedly charmed half the female population of New York City—and then he left. Leaving Sarah in a position she hadn't been in before with Caleb Lewis.

Out of control.

Caleb should have been glad that of all people, the reporter who had been his nemesis had been the one to lose the Frederick K. He could call it karmic payback for writing all those stories about his personal life.

Sarah Griffin had created an image of him— one nearly everyone believed—as a womanizing, shallow man. One more concerned about the blonde on his arm than the bottom line.

She didn't know the truth—no one did—about why he filled his nights with the mindless world of nightclubs. Why he chose to forget his mistakes by spinning through relationships like an errant top.

When he'd walked into the magazine's offices earlier today, he'd had no intention of talking to any of the reporters who worked for the tabloid side of the magazine. Especially not Sarah Griffin. It wasn't that he didn't like her—he barely knew her—or find her attractive—because she was beautiful, quite so—it was more that he wanted to avoid the person who had painted him with a one-dimensional brush.

He had seen Sarah Griffin dozens of times, in the background of the clubs he frequented, the restaurants where he dined. She avoided the spotlight that shone on him, never taking off the reporter hat to have a drink or take a spin on the dance floor. That didn't stop him from noticing the quiet, observant woman in his periphery. Her wide green eyes took in everything he did and said, then her poisoned pen pasted all that information on the next issue's pages. He often wondered how she was judging him—though all he had to do was open the latest issue to find out.

If it were any other day—and any other circumstances—he would have been intrigued by a woman like Sarah. Her slender frame held the kind of curves that said she enjoyed food and didn't spend her days subsisting on diet soda and cigarettes. Her brown hair hung in a long, sleek curtain down her back, with a couple of loose tendrils curling around the edges of the bronze-rimmed frames of her glasses. She had an understated beauty about her, one not augmented by the artifice of overdone makeup and overbright hair dye. She was very much a what-you-see-is-what-you-get kind of woman.

For Caleb, who had met far too many of the illusion-is-my-middle-name kind of women, Sarah's fresh-faced looks were refreshing. Intriguing.

Except for the fact that she'd written half the stories that lambasted him and painted him as a carousing devil—she could be the kind of woman he'd date. Still, hadn't he learned from watching his mother's own heartbreak that a reporter could turn on a subject in an instant, all in the quest for that immortal headline?

But, as he had crossed the room full of the writers' cubicles, he'd realized bringing Sarah Griffin around to his side could serve him in more than one way. If he could convince her to do a story on LL Designs, maybe she'd see another side of him and of the company. And in the process, he hoped he could convince her to stop trotting his personal life through the "Seen and Heard" pages of the magazine.

What was that old saying? Keep your friends close and your enemies closer? Over the years, Sarah Griffin had definitely become an enemy of sorts. Keeping her close seemed like a good idea. Despite the trash she was in charge of penning, he had to admit—grudgingly—that she was the best writer at the publication. Whether he agreed with them or not, her stories were witty, punchy and memorable. Exactly the kind of piece he needed for LL Designs.

Then he'd seen the poster for the missing shoe.

Jackpot.

With the shoe as leverage, he could surely get Sarah's attention, be able to work out some kind of deal, encouraging her to be more amenable to writing a favorable-to-the-company article. Maybe convince her he wasn't the bad boy she thought he was and see how writing an in-depth story on LL Designs' new season could benefit them both.

Who better to understand and appreciate his launching of a shoe line than the woman who was in possession of the debut pair of Frederick Ks? At the same time, it hadn't taken him long to realize working with her meant bringing her into the office—and risking that she would see the missing Frederick K on his desk. He could just see the headline now: Desperate Business Owner Swipes competitor's Newest Design.

Yeah, not the kind of press Caleb was looking for.

Still, it was a chance he was willing to take. He had a feeling this could be a very beneficial arrangement for his business.

He reached up, grabbed the shoe and shoved it into one of the drawers of his desk. He would tell her he had the stiletto—but after he had a chance to explain what had happened, and make Sarah Griffin see he wasn't as bad as her headlines painted him.

The numbers on his office clock had just flipped to 2:00 p.m. when Martha buzzed Caleb. "You have a visitor," she said.

Caleb chuckled. Right on time. He wasn't surprised. Sarah Griffin was probably completely freaked out about the missing stiletto. Losing something like that—particularly when the issue's deadline was right around the corner—had to have her stomach in knots. And to lose one of the ultra-secret Frederick Ks? If her job wasn't already on the line, it would be soon.

And that gave Caleb leverage. "Send her right in," he said.

"Uh, it's not a her."

Not a her? Had Sarah Griffin sent someone

else in her stead? Or had she decided he was bluffing about the shoe and just blown him off?

His door opened and a heavyset man in a bright blue suit stepped inside. He stood about six feet tall and half that in width, with a shock of short white hair that stood out in a cloud-shaped halo around his head. Beneath the suit he wore a red-and-white striped button-down shirt, complete with a matching pocket square. There was nothing about the man that said simple, understated or pay-me-no-mind. Not his clothing, not his mannerisms and definitely not his infamous booming voice. "Hello, Caleb."

"Frederick. How nice to see you."

The flamboyant owner of Frederick K designs chuckled. "Don't lie, my boy. We all know you hate my guts." He crossed the room and stopped by one of the visitor's chairs but didn't sit down. Probably avoiding wrinkles in his perfectly pressed bright-blue suit.

Caleb rose, and came around to lean on the edge of his desk. "Let me guess. You're here because you've realized this fashion business is just too competitive for you and you want me to buy you out."

Frederick K snorted. "That'll be the day. Oh, no, I'm here to offer you the opposite." He leaned in, his dark-brown gaze meeting Caleb's. "I want to buy *you* out. Lock, stock and barrel."

The offer came as a surprise to Caleb but he didn't betray that emotion. Why would successful Frederick K want to take over struggling LL Designs? Was it merely to eliminate a little more of the competition? "I'm not for sale. And neither is this company."

Frederick K laughed, the sound hearty, coming from somewhere deep in that expansive gut of his. "You'd rather file bankruptcy?"

"We're fine."

Another laugh. "My, my. You are delusional." Frederick reached into the inside breast pocket of his suit, withdrew a sheet of paper and fluttered it onto Caleb's desk. "My offer. Sign it, and you're released from this—" Frederick waved a hand. "—prison of your mother's making."

A tide of anger rose in Caleb's chest. Give up his mother's company? Sell her decades of hard work to this buffoon? "I will never sell to you. I won't sell you so much as a thread of my mother's company."

"I always thought you were a bad businessman, but never a fool." Frederick K shook his head, making the white cloud dance. "And I'm so rarely wrong."

Caleb pushed off from his desk and towered over the other man. "Get out of my office."

"I'll see you at the shows in a couple of weeks," Frederick K said. "Unless of course you're smart enough to quit while you're behind." He gestured again toward the slip of paper.

"I'll be there," Caleb said. "And LL Designs will be the one getting the buzz this year. Not Frederick K."

"Delusional," Frederick K muttered again, under his breath, then he walked out of Caleb's office. Caleb was tempted to slam and lock the door behind him, but he didn't.

The man had been right. He'd taken the pulse of LL Designs, and found it weakening by the day. A smart businessman would have taken the offer of a buyout, pocketed the cash and walked away. Then this entire burden would be on someone else's shoulders and he'd be free to pursue his own career again, rather than the one he'd inherited.

He could be free. Of the worries. The stresses. The too-heavy burden of being CEO.

Caleb picked up the single sheet from Frederick K, dropped into his office chair again—

And sent the paper through the shredder.

The elevator seemed to take its sweet time bringing Sarah to the top floor of the steel-and-glass building that housed LL Designs. She'd hemmed and hawed for a good ten minutes about whether or not Caleb Lewis had been serious or just looking for a way to get back at her for all the gossip columns. Either way, she couldn't be sure without taking him up on his offer.

Offer, ha. It had been a dare, couched in friendly terms.

He wanted to see if she was willing to step into the lion's den to find out if he had her missing stiletto. It was possible, she had reasoned, that the entire thing was a set-up. That Caleb Lewis had used the wanted poster to formulate a ruse that would make a fool out of her. And in the process, exact a little revenge for all those columns.

But then she came back to the look on his face when he had seen the poster. He knew something—and she was not leaving here until she found out what it was.

The elevator doors opened. Sarah's steps stuttered when she saw who was waiting for the car.

Frederick K.

The designer was talking on his phone—barking into it, really—and didn't even notice her as she passed by him and into the corridor. Not that he ever had. Frederick K was the kind of guy who talked to his people, and told them to talk to all the "other" people. Those who existed beneath his stratosphere.

Had he been here about the shoe? Had Caleb Lewis double-crossed her? After the elevator doors closed behind Frederick K, Sarah breezed straight into Caleb's office, bypassing his assistant's desk over the woman's objections. "Did you sell me out?"

Caleb stared at her. "Sell you out? To whom? For what?"

"I just saw Frederick K leaving here. Did you tell him?"

"About the shoe you lost?" A grin darted across Caleb's face. "Now, why would I do that?"

"Because that's the kind of man you are."

The grin disappeared, replaced by a scowl. "You have me all wrong."

"I wrote the stories, Mr. Lewis. I did the research. I know you."

He came around his desk, until mere inches separated them. His woodsy cologne teased at her senses, tempting her to draw closer.

She didn't.

"You're wrong, Miss Griffin," he said, his voice low and quiet. "I'm not the man you have portrayed on your pages."

His gaze met hers, and her thoughts stammered to a stop. Every time she came into contact with the owner of LL Designs, Sarah forgot her own name, never mind what she was going to say.

He had a way of riveting his attention on her, making her feel like no one else existed in his world at that moment except her. But she knew better—she herself had put together the gossip pages that linked Caleb Lewis to every runway model in a five-mile radius. A smart woman would avoid entangling herself with a man like him. He had *heartbreaker* written all over his face.

"Why am I here?" she asked. "If this is some kind of ruse—"

"Don't you want to know where that shoe is?"

Did he have it? Or know something she didn't? Her heart skipped a beat. She put a smile on her face, hoping diplomacy would bring him over to her side—and get her the information on the stiletto that much faster. "I know my articles on you haven't been that flattering, and I appreciate you being so understanding about this shoe… fiasco."

He perched on the edge of his desk and crossed his arms over his chest. "I never said I had it or that I would give it back, just like that." He snapped his fingers.

Damn. He must have the stiletto. Then why wouldn't he admit it?

What did he want?

"One shoe doesn't do you any good, Mr. Lewis. Certainly—"

"Quid pro quo, Miss Griffin. You want something and so do I."

She glared at him. "If this is some twisted way of propositioning me, I assure you—"

Laughter burst from him. "I assure you, this is not about sex."

Her ego smarted at the words, and heat climbed her neck. Well, geez. He didn't have to be so blunt about it.

Why did she care what he thought about her? She had no desire to be part of Caleb Lewis's model harem. But still...

It'd be nice to have him notice her. Just for ego's sake. That was all.

"I want ink," he said.

"Ink?" She pushed her glasses up on her nose, acutely aware that in her jeans and dark-brown cowl-neck sweater she didn't exactly scream sex goddess. Surrounded by images of the stunning women who wore LL Designs' latest creations, she felt out of her element. Particularly with Caleb Lewis zeroing so much of his attention on her. Attention that clearly had nothing to do with sexual desires.

Was that because her brown sweater made her look about as sexy as a loaf of bread? Or simply that Caleb was sticking to business only? Still, his questions, his directness, unnerved her. Sarah was usually the one behind the scenes— not the one in the scene. "Isn't that what Office Depot is for?"

"I don't mean printer ink," Caleb said. "I mean a story. On my company."

Suspicion rose inside her again. He knew what she'd written—surely he read *Behind the Scenes*—why would he want her, of all people, to write the story on his company? One that he undoubtedly expected would put a positive spin on the struggling design firm?

"Why me?"

He leaned forward. "Because contrary to some of the...fluff—" In his tone she heard the struggle to use a euphemism for his true feelings about those columns. "—you have published in the past, you are the best writer on staff over there. And though I may have disagreed a time or ten with what you've written about me," at this, a grin whispered across his face, then disappeared so quickly she wasn't even sure it had been a genuine smile, "I have found your writing to be smart and witty."

The compliments washed over her, settling into the insecure cracks in her writer persona.

She didn't care if someone was the most successful writer or painter in the world, there was just something about the creative spirit that was more vulnerable than that of, say, an accountant. She'd obsessed about every story she'd ever written, always sure her editor was going to kick it back with a big red REJECTED stamp across the top.

"Thank you."

"Don't thank me yet, Miss Griffin. There's an addendum to this offer."

"Mr. Lewis—"

"Call me Caleb, please." That grin danced across his features again, and Sarah's stomach did a little flip-flop. "I feel like my grandfather when you say that."

"Caleb." His name slid off her tongue. Too easily. "The editorial calendar is set months in advance and I can't—"

He pushed off from the desk and closed the gap between them. He was so close, she could see that his eyes—which she'd always thought were just blue—were a tempting combination of blue-gray, like the sky just after a storm cleared. She didn't recognize his cologne, but resisted the urge to inhale the deep, musky notes. "If you wanted to badly enough, you could."

Could what? Kiss him? Because some insane part of her wanted to do that. Pretty darn badly.

Especially the way he looked today—in a white button-down shirt open at the collar, the crimson tie tugged down just enough to expose a tempting V of his neck. He'd taken off his suit jacket and draped it over the back of his chair. The simple deletion had transformed him, and the relaxed, almost cavalier tone to his attire made her want to see what would happen if she unknotted that tie, then slipped each one of those tiny white buttons out of their holes and—

She cleared her throat and moved back. "No can do. I'm sorry."

Really sorry. She'd have done about anything to see him grin again. No wonder the models gushed about him as though he was a movie star. He had the kind of charm that tempted a woman to drop her guard, expose a chink in the walls around her heart, and go after him with wild abandon. She'd watched him from afar a thousand times, but up close—

Up close, he exerted a raw sexuality that said he would be very, very good in bed. Oh, boy.

"I'm sorry," she said again, "but I'm not willing to compromise my ethics and just write some pretty little ego-stroking piece about you to counteract any bad press you may have received."

He scowled. "This isn't about me."

"Then what is it about?"

"The company. I want a story written on LL Designs. Showcasing the company in a way your publication hasn't done for years. I promise, it'll be a great exclusive."

For a second, she thought of another kind of exclusive—the kind where Caleb Lewis paid attention to her and no one else. The kind where she spent her evenings with him parked in front of a roaring fire, exploring every delicious inch of his tall, broad frame. And him doing the same to her, over and over again.

Get a grip, Sarah. The last thing you need is a relationship with a man like him.

And the last person a man like him would go for was someone like her. She wasn't leggy or glamorous. She was...just Sarah. Nothing wrong with that, but nothing spectacular about it, either.

"I don't know," she said. "How do I know you'll make this story worth my while?"

"I have something you need." He paused. "The missing Frederick K stiletto."

The shoe. He *did* have it.

All the years she'd worked at *Behind the Scenes,* Sarah had done her job—and done it well—and figured a promotion to the inside pages, to the real meat and potatoes of *Smart Fashion,* was only a matter of time. Then she could write real articles about real topics, instead of covering how many drinks some model had before she made a fool out of herself on a tabletop.

Except that hadn't happened. Karl had kept her glued to the gossip pages, tossing her the occasional accessory story, a paragraph or two on new handbags and nail polishes for the "What's New" column at *Smart Fashion,* all the while promising "someday" she'd move to the regular magazine, dangling it like a carrot on a string. She'd despaired of ever writing anything remotely meaningful.

Until one of the main writers for the fashion pages, Betsy Wilkins, had pitched a hissy fit in the middle of a photo shoot over the way her piece was edited, and Karl had ordered her out of the building. The writers' pit had still been buzzing about the dramatic exit when Karl strode down the hall, dumped the shoes on Sarah's desk and said, "don't screw it up."

Not exactly the rousing endorsement of her future she'd hoped for. For five seconds, Sarah had panicked, sure she wasn't up to covering the famous designer's spring designs.

Then she'd taken a closer look at the shoes, and in them, seen an opportunity for much more than career advancement. Rather, a chance for a real change. The kind she had dreamed of ever since she'd first picked up a pen and imagined herself as a journalist. She'd gotten derailed from that dream for a little, but now she was back on track, thanks to the perfect-size designer shoes.

Half of which were in Caleb Lewis's possession.

He put out his hand. "Do we have a deal?"

"What deal are you proposing?"

"It's simple. You give me what I want, and I give you what you want." His gaze met hers. "Everybody wins."

She had dealt with the worst of the modeling world's personalities. Covered stories no one wanted her to cover. Surely she could work with Caleb Lewis and not get swept up in his blue eyes and easy charm.

After all, she knew him. And knew he had about as much sticking power for relationships as a wet piece of tape. She'd be smart, not starry-eyed.

"You have a deal, Mr. Lewis," she said and took his hand. When they touched, a zing ran through her.

Which told Sarah Griffin this "deal" wasn't going to be the uncomplicated arrangement she'd hoped.

Not at all.

CHAPTER THREE

"FIRST, we need some ground rules," Caleb said. He had paused outside the doors to his factory, one hand on the lever, the other lingering behind Sarah's back. As if he was guiding her inside, but half of him had to admit it was so he had an excuse to touch her again.

When they had shaken hands a moment ago, he'd felt it—that little quiver of electricity running through his body, lighting up senses that Caleb had been sure had gone dark forever. He'd been with some of the most beautiful women in the world and never felt a tenth of the electricity he'd felt when he'd taken Sarah Griffin's hand.

Why? Was it because she challenged him on every level? Because of their built-in animosity over her column? One of those push-pull attraction kind of things?

But more to the point, what the hell was he doing? She was the enemy. Not a woman he wanted to—or should—get close to. He had to guard the secrets in his life, and guard them well, especially around a gossip reporter. Except every time he looked into her deep green eyes, he seemed to forget that.

"Ground rules?" A half laugh escaped her. "Don't you trust me?"

"Frankly, no." He gestured toward the copy of *Behind the Scenes* that was sitting on top of a pile of magazines spilling out of the recycle bin. Right there on the cover, in bold red letters, were the words she had written. Fashion's Hottest Bad Boy Exposed. He tapped the cover. "Did this help you sell more issues?"

"It didn't hurt." She turned toward him, which broke the contact of his hand on her back. "I'm sorry, but that's the truth."

He could just see the people standing in the checkout line, picking up the tabloid and plunking down their few dollars to devour the petty details of his life. Get the people to buy the publication, by any means, then hope they read the ads and buy the products splashed on the pages.

He understood the chess game of marketing and sales. Hell, he was one of those advertisers hoping to get noticed by the reader. Didn't mean he liked being one of the pawns, though.

"Number one," Caleb said. "There will be no

more of these kinds of articles done on me while we are working together."

"You can't—"

"Find someone else to focus your attention on. Someone besides 'Devil-May-Care Caleb.'" The last few words ended with a note of distaste.

She arched a brow and a tease lit her gaze. "Well, there's a problem with that. I don't know another Devil-May-Care CEO." Her smile widened. Sarah Griffin clearly wasn't daunted by him, at all. Despite everything, he liked that. A lot. "Do you know a lot of playboy bachelor CEOs in the fashion industry? Is there, like, a club for you guys?"

He laughed, the sound exploding from his chest. After the stress of the last few weeks— hell, months—laughter felt good. "Oh, yeah. There's a support group and everything."

"And what's your motto?" Her green eyes danced with merriment. "If it ain't on the front page, it ain't worth doing?"

"I see you've been to one of our meetings."

She laughed. He liked the sound. Light and fresh, like a spring breeze. "Where do you think I get all my ideas for the gossip column?"

A slight flush accentuated her delicate features, peaked in her cheeks and drew his attention down to her full lips. For a second, he forgot everything that had happened between them.

Forgot that she was the enemy. Forgot that he was supposed to be focused on the company, not her. All he could think about was kissing those soft pink lips and hearing her soft laughter of joy against his mouth.

Whoa. Back the horse up, cowboy, and get back to business.

And don't trust a reporter. Ever.

Still, a part of him—the part that was urging him to kiss her—was whispering that he could trust Sarah. Could get close to her.

"Let's, uh, hope what you see today gives you an idea for something else to write about." He pushed on the double doors to the factory, and gestured for her to enter. He took a step, then paused just inside the room. Didn't matter how many times he came down to the sixty-thousand-square-foot factory, the sheer power of the massive space always brought him to a standstill. Dozens of people, working fabric, needles, thread, all in perfect synchronization, producing what some would view as works of art. Taking one designer's vision and transforming it into a reality, one dress, one skirt, one pair of slacks at a time.

"Amazing," she said quietly.

"This is going to sound crazy, but I think the same thing every time I come down here. I used to come here with my mother on Saturdays when

I was a little boy. It was cool then, because everything was quiet and still. But my favorite days were the weekdays when this place was humming like a beehive."

"It is like that, isn't it? A beehive?"

"Yep. And the queen bee, she used to really keep things hopping here." Caleb chuckled at the memory. "My mother would get it in her head that her collection really needed to feature teal and miniskirts, and wham, the lines would have to switch gears so she could add this new idea to the mix."

"She's a brilliant designer. One of the true pioneers in fashion."

"Thank you." A few quiet words, and a bridge formed between them. One he hadn't expected or asked for. But there it was.

He should say something back. Instead, he retreated into his comfort zone.

Work.

Caleb stopped by the cutting table, watching as a worker unfurled a thick roll of satiny robin's-egg-blue fabric. He rolled it back and forth several times, stacking layer upon layer before pushing a button and watching as the cutting tool came down and computer cut out the pieces for a dress.

"This is for our ready-to-wear collection," Caleb explained above the whir and whoosh of the machine. "The mass-market pieces that end up in major department stores. Many of our couture pieces are still handmade, from start to finish."

"This will be the Danube dress, won't it?" Sarah asked, pointing at the stack of cut pieces already being loaded onto a transfer cart for the next step in the process.

He nodded, pleased that she knew the collection well enough to recognize a piece at the assembly stage. "And what do you think of it?"

"Well, I..." She waved a hand vaguely instead of answering the question.

"Let me guess. 'Lacking in originality, this year's collection from LL Designs is unfocused and flashy. Much like the company's owner.'"

She pushed her glasses up on her nose. "I only write the truth."

"You call that truth?" The bridge between them dissolved, putting them right back into choppy waters. Confronting her was probably not his wisest course of action. He needed her on his side—not working against him. But he couldn't seem to find the governor for his mouth. "That's just an excuse for those ridiculous headlines."

Sarah propped a fist on her hip. "Listen, I could easily write pieces that stroke your ego and make your company seem like the next best thing since sliced bread. But I can't. And I won't."

He snorted. "Why?" He had to raise his voice to be heard above the constant whir of the sewing machines. "Journalistic integrity getting in the way? Or the rush to get the story in print before some other tabloid does?"

She chewed on her upper lip, and he knew he'd ticked her off. Damn. This was going all wrong. He was supposed to impress her with the factory, with the amazing productivity of his workers, with the new designs launching this year.

"It's not like that," she said.

"Oh, yeah? Well, it sure feels like that on my end."

She threw up her hands. "Listen, I didn't come here for you to leap all over me about my columns. I'm sorry you aren't happy with them, but I don't answer to you. Why don't you just give me back the shoe and we'll both admit this isn't going to work out?"

He could do that. He could take the easy road out. Find another reporter at the magazine to work with. There were at least a dozen on staff there, and he could surely find one person who would be easier to work with. Nicer.

Except, he was never going to get Sarah Griffin to stop writing those pieces if he didn't show her he wasn't the devil in a suit she thought he was. He had a prime opportunity to foster a new kind of relationship with the press.

Martha had been right. Caleb hadn't been nice to the reporters, and he hadn't exactly given them much to write about *besides* his love life. If he wanted to change the headlines, he needed to change his approach.

Starting with his own reactions to her words. He bit back his pride. "What is it about the company's latest designs that you find so..." He paused before forcing the words out a second time. "'Unfocused and lacking in originality'?"

She eyed him. "You want my honest opinion?"

As much as he wanted to say no, he didn't. The company was in trouble, and had been ever since he took over. He'd welcome any light shed on why. Even from Sarah Griffin. "Yes, I do."

She took a step closer to the cutting table, where a second bolt of fabric—this time in a pale spring green—was being unrolled. "The one thing LL Designs used to be known for when your mother was in charge was taking chances. For not answering to anyone. The company didn't follow trends. It set them."

He nodded. He had read those words more than once about his mother's fashion sense and approach to doing business. "My mother was amazing at her job."

"And over the last year," Sarah went on, "it seems like the company has lost its focus. Like you're throwing every design you can out there and trying to see what sticks."

She'd nailed him, in just a few words. Taken what he and his staff had been dancing around for months and brought it all together with an outsider's laser beam. She surprised him, because he'd expected her to say something about his lack of personal focus or his late nights cutting into his concentration. Sarah Griffin was a smarter cookie than he had expected.

The problem was figuring out how to do anything different. He knew the collections weren't hitting the mark—he just hadn't figured out how to make them what they once were. "We're lacking vision. Focus," he said.

She nodded. "Like with the Danube dress. It's pretty. But so are thousands of other dresses this season. Scalloped neck, cap sleeves, tea length. Classic, something a woman might wear to an outdoor party."

"And there's something wrong with that?"

Her gaze went to some far-off place. "What a woman wants is to be remembered," she said quietly. "To know that when she walks into a room, people are going to notice her." Then she backed away a bit from the table and cleared her throat, as if putting distance between herself and the subject at hand. "Well, most women, anyway."

Caleb glanced over at Sarah's chocolate-brown sweater and dark jeans. A plain outfit, nothing that screamed "notice me." "Not all women, huh?"

"Some of us like our life in the shadows."

"I don't see you as a shadows kind of woman."

She drew herself up. "I'm not here to analyze my life, Mr. Lewis."

"We're back to that again? What happened to Caleb?" A part of him liked teasing her, if only to see the consternation that whisked across her features. It wasn't about getting her back for all the times she'd written about him—it was about figuring out what made this woman tick. She was strong, opinionated and not afraid of a little confrontation. Yet she seemed to want to avoid anything personal. She had up a hell of a wall and the intrigued part of Caleb wanted to know why.

"Caleb," she corrected, and he loved the way the two syllables of his name slid off her tongue, "I'm here to learn about your business. Not talk about me."

"But I think talking about you helps my business."

She laughed. "Right."

"You are part of my core consumer group." Okay, so that was partly a lie. Right now, he didn't care at all about Sarah being part of a focus group. He was more interested in what she thought and why—about more than just the dress on the cutting table.

About him.

Oh, he was treading in some dangerous waters. The very ones he had tried so hard to avoid.

"Like I have a couture budget?" Sarah said. "I don't think so."

"The ready-to-wear collection is carried in department stores nationwide. Stores you undoubtedly shop in regularly."

"Still, I don't think—"

"Oh, but I do," he interrupted. The tables had turned, and Caleb had to admit he was enjoying this game. Very much. "In fact, I think we should talk about this over lunch."

"I really don't think—"

"I do. It'll give us a quieter place to talk than the factory floor."

Wary unease filled her face and he wondered if he'd pushed her too far. "If this is some kind of date…"

"It's not." Though a part of him wondered what it would be like to date Sarah Griffin. To kiss that sassy mouth until she was moaning against him, and saying nothing more than his name. To take her in his arms, and run his touch down her hourglass figure. To find out if she was just as direct and strong in the bedroom as she was right now.

"Business only?" She held up her reporter's pad.

"Of course. Why would I think anything else?" And he smiled right through that lie.

Sarah hadn't been this aware of a man in...forever. She sat beside Caleb Lewis in the cramped, cigar-stinking interior of the cab and tried to keep her thoughts on the story. On the information she would need to gather to do an incisive piece on LL Designs.

The right story could get Karl to see she was more than a gossip reporter. That she belonged at the magazine, not at the tabloid. Maybe even get her Betsy's position on a permanent basis. Or better yet, the spot of top writer.

What she needed was a hook. Something that would capture the reader's attention and make her story a must-read.

—Like the hook of the sexy CEO running

the company. That would get every woman's attention. It did mine.

An angle that was different from all the here's-what-company-ABC-is-doing-this-spring pieces she'd read before.

—What was that cologne he was wearing? God, it smelled so good. Like the woods after a rain storm.

Something that would make her article stand out. Make her boss realize she could be a fabulous reporter, one who deserved more than a few rumor-riddled pages in the tabloid.

—Does he work out? Because he sure looks like he does. The way that shirt fits him, skimming over the muscles in his arm...

Stop it, Sarah. The job, the story. Focus on those. Not him.

She turned in her seat to face him, which put a couple inches of distance between them. Not enough. Not nearly enough. Because she was still acutely aware of his every move.

"Why did you take the shoe?" she asked. "I mean, you must have known it was a Frederick K as soon as you saw it on the ground."

"I did. And to say I was surprised to find a designer stiletto on the ground beside a trash can would be an understatement."

"My sister had a...temper tantrum," Sarah

said. "Except she's twenty-two, and technically, I think she's too old for temper tantrums."

"Tell that to the models," Caleb said.

Sarah laughed. "True."

The cab stopped for a red light. A family of five—mom, dad, three little girls—crossed in front of the cab, the children following behind like ducklings in matching red plaid coats. "I picked up the shoe because I wanted to know what Frederick K knew that I didn't," Caleb said. "Ever since he came on the scene, his business has been booming on a thousand levels, and mine...hasn't. I thought maybe analyzing his newest venture might give me a peek inside what has made him so successful."

The honesty surprised her. He could have said anything—he was going to look for its rightful owner, he'd thought it would make a great gag, he wasn't going to keep it at all—but instead he'd been truthful with her.

"And did you figure out those answers?" she asked.

"I'm working on it." They'd entered a maze of stop-and-go traffic, a cacophony of engine sounds and beeping horns. The taxi driver had turned on a radio station and the high-pitched strains of foreign music carried inside the car. "Can I ask you something?"

"Sure."

"What would you think about LL Designs going into the shoe business? It's the most logical step, pardon the pun, in expanding our business. And it's been a successful venture for other designers."

"You mean like Frederick K."

"More or less, yes."

She thought a moment, picturing the last few years of offerings from LL Designs. The company had always concentrated a good portion of its business on skirts and dresses, making a shoe line a logical choice. "I think it would be a good fit."

"Only if the shoes are boring and plain, right?" He gave her a teasing grin.

"No, not at all."

"Why do you say that? I mean, your analysis of LL Designs hasn't exactly been flattering recently. What makes you think we can hit this one out of the park?"

"The company may have fumbled for the last few seasons, but I think it has potential," Sarah said. "LL Designs was an industry leader before, and I'm sure you will be there again."

"If the CEO smartens up?"

"Your words," she said, and smiled again.

But they were true words. He needed to get a clue about where he was going wrong. Sarah, he realized, had a good handle on the industry, despite being constrained to the gossip pages. As they rode, he asked her about the current trends that she was seeing in the magazine, and as Sarah told him about the rise in Old World-style decorations and a deeper palette of colors, she found herself enjoying the attention. Not just of Caleb Lewis's deep blue eyes on her face, but of someone who cared what she thought about something other than the latest model throwing a tantrum story. He was interested in her opinions, her thoughts, her theories.

The attention was intoxicating, exciting. It reminded her of why she'd gone into the field of writing in the beginning. Because she wanted to share what she thought. Have a voice in the world around her.

Had she been behind the scenes, reporting on other people's lives like some kind of voyeur with a pen, for too long? Allowed herself to get caught in a rut? Maybe. After all, she'd started at *Behind the Scenes* when she was in college, working part-time in the mail room, then moving up to the writers' pit once she had her journalism degree. She'd always imagined leaving someday, and working for the kind of hard-hitting journalism publications that had inspired her to go into reporting in the first place.

And thus far, she'd done nothing more than

write about people's love lives and ugly divorces. Yeah, way to go on those career goals.

No more, Sarah had decided that day she had taken the shoes home. She was tired of living in the shadows of her life, her career. When she'd shoved the stilettos into her bag, she'd embarked on the beginnings of a change—one that she hadn't had a chance to execute before the lone Frederick K disappeared. Shoes or no shoes, she refused to spend one more day living the same life as she had before. That meant talking business with Caleb Lewis, sharing a meal with him in public, allowing the man to know a part of her. Becoming a part of the world she used to just write about.

"Although the new big thing is muted colors like grays and browns, I think the trend is going to be bright colors. Shoes that scream 'look at me.' Women pay a lot of money for shoes because they want people to look at them, and I just don't see this muted color thing hanging around long."

Caleb leaned in closer to her, and at the same time the cab turned right, closing the distance between them even further. She inhaled his cologne, caught sight of the faint shadow of stubble along his jawline, and wondered for one long second what it would be like to kiss him in that very spot.

"Then what do your footwear choices say about you?" He gestured at her feet, at the flat black leather boots she had paired with her jeans. They were plain, ordinary and exactly the opposite of what she'd been talking about. She'd had the pair for years, and their position as her favorite work shoes showed in the wear and tear on the soles.

"These?" She laughed. "These are practical."

"Is that the real reason you wear them? Or, as you just pointed out, do you want the opposite? For people *not* to notice you?"

"I'd rather be noticed for my mind than my shoes." Except a part of her wanted people to see her walk into a room and think, *wow.* The way they had always reacted to Diana, the one who had worn the fancy pink dresses and sparkly ballet slippers. Kinda hard to be the center of attention, though, with just her brain and a pair of scuffed boots.

"Shoes or not," Caleb said, his voice low and dark and his gaze locked on hers, "I noticed. You."

The sentence, broken apart like that into two separate ones, rocketed through her. He'd noticed her. Paid attention to the details. It made her wonder what he would have done if she looked like one of those models he dated. With the windswept hair and pouty red lips, the triple coats of mascara and breast-enhancing bras.

"And tell me, Mr. Lewis," she said, reverting to the distance of using his last name, "is being noticed by you a good thing or a bad thing?"

CHAPTER FOUR

THE restaurant had been a bad choice. What had he been thinking?

That maybe he'd impress the sassy reporter with his choice of a "hot spot"? Yeah, not so much, if the annoyance on Sarah Griffin's face was any indication of his success rate. If anything, he'd achieved the opposite result.

"Caleb!" The third model in the last ten minutes came by his table, brushing air kisses onto both his cheeks. Her floral perfume flooded his senses, shoving his nostrils into a garden of lilies. "It's been so long since I've seen you! We should do lunch!"

He murmured something that sounded like assent, then, thankfully, the model saw someone more important and more interesting, and she breezed off, calling out a greeting to the movie producer across the room.

"Well, you're certainly popular," Sarah said. "Perhaps lunch was a bad idea."

"I promise, I'm all yours. Cindy Crawford herself could come by and I'd just ignore her." Caleb shot Sarah a grin.

It didn't work its usual magic. If anything, Sarah Griffin seemed completely immune to his charms. Sure, she'd smiled a few times at him, but that wasn't the same as flirting, or returning his attempts to flirt. He couldn't remember the last time he'd been involved with a woman who challenged him. Who made him work for her attention. Sarah Griffin didn't seem to be the least bit attracted to him. A smarter man would take that as a sign just to let it go.

He shouldn't have cared—after all, she had written all those awful stories about him—but for some reason, it mattered to Caleb that Sarah saw him in a different light than the one cast on him by the gossip pages.

Okay, so the last ten minutes hadn't exactly helped his case.

"Let's get out of here," he said.

"I thought you wanted to get something to eat."

"This environment isn't exactly conducive to conversation." He rose, dropped a few bills on the table, then waited for Sarah to join him. "We'll grab a bite somewhere else."

If she had reservations about the change of plans, she didn't voice them. Instead, she followed him out of the restaurant and onto the streets of New York. He hailed a cab, and a minute later they were speeding toward the shopping district. "Before we eat, I want to show you something."

"Okay." A little doubt edged the tone of her voice.

The cab slowed in front of a small boutique on a busy corner. A brightly colored awning hung a semicircular greeting over the antique front door. As they walked inside, a small bell tinkled a greeting. It was a cozy shop, filled with bright colors, several small loveseats and a half dozen antique standing mirrors. Caleb had always admired the combination of cozy with chic. This was the kind of shop New York was famous for—as far from department-store shopping as one could get.

As Caleb crossed the room, a small Asian woman slipped out from behind the counter. "Nice to see you again, Mr. Lewis."

He gave the woman a smile and shook her hand. "How's business, Lia?"

"Just fine, just fine." She waved at the half dozen or so customers milling about the shop. The quiet sound of hangers sliding over racks punctuated conversations. "There's been plenty of activity, and from what I've been hearing, people are looking forward to next season's models, too."

"Great." He gestured to Sarah, and she moved next to him, but not close enough to touch him. "This is Sarah Griffin, a reporter with the fashion industry. I thought I'd give her a little insider peek at how my business works."

Lia arched a brow in interest, and probably in the hopes of some free publicity for her shop. "That's wonderful. If you're going to pick a subject, Mr. Lewis is a great one. I've dealt with a lot of fashion houses, and his is…different."

"Really? How?" Sarah fished her reporter's pad out of her purse, and clicked on a pen. Clearly intrigued.

Caleb drifted away from the two women, figuring that Lia would feel more comfortable talking about him and his company if he wasn't standing right there. He stood to the side, watching the shoppers go through the racks. One woman—mid-thirties, he guessed, and wearing an A-line skirt and light green floral-print cardigan—stopped by a rack filled with this season's dresses from LL Designs. He watched her fingers skip over the hangers as she sorted through the different choices, past this one, then that one, pausing at another. She selected a camel-colored sheath, held it to her chest, considering it for a long moment. Just when Caleb thought she might buy the dress, the woman slipped it back onto the rack and moved on to the next rack of clothes—ones from another designer.

Damn.

He was watching the exact problem he was having with declining profits in action. Frustration brimmed inside him. He couldn't force people to buy the clothes from LL Designs, and if he cornered the woman and asked her why she hadn't bought the dress, chances were she'd think he was crazy. And even if she did answer him, he'd bet she'd say she couldn't quite tell him what it had been that had tipped the scales into the no arena. Personal purchases were emotional decisions, and clearly, he wasn't hitting the right emotions.

"Well, you have a fan here," Sarah said, slipping in beside him.

"Lia is a great customer. She's been buying LL Designs since the day she opened." Caleb sent the shop owner a wave, then held the door for Sarah as they left the shop. The afternoon sun hit them with a welcome blast of soft warmth, tempered by the noisy hum of a city at work. Taxis hurrying to their destinations, people entering and exiting buildings, delivery trucks stopping and starting along their routes.

The scents of roast beef, honey ham and spicy

mustard drifted from a mobile sandwich truck half a block away. "What's your favorite?"

She smiled. "Pastrami on rye. Not the best choice for my hips, but try telling that to my stomach."

Caleb chuckled. "A woman after my own heart. Don't tell my doctor, but that's my favorite, too."

A smile extended between them, a connection. The world seemed to drop away, the noises fading into the background, the stresses of a moment ago gone for now. All Caleb saw was the curve of Sarah's lips, the way her smile seemed to light her eyes, her face.

"Sir? Can I help you?"

The question jolted Caleb back to the present. "Uh, two pastrami on rye, please." He fished the money out of his pocket, paid the man, then took the sandwiches and handed one to Sarah. They both added mustard, which elicited another of those connecting smiles, then stepped back to eat their sandwiches.

"Lia had really nice things to say about you," Sarah said. "Things that..." her voice trailed off.

"Surprised you?"

She shrugged, then nodded. "I had no idea you were so hands-on with the shops that carry your clothes. She said you come in there regularly to see how things are going, to ask her opinion and get her feedback."

"She's the one dealing directly with the public. It's better than asking a bunch of suits what they think, or pulling in some random focus group. You want answers, go directly to the source."

"Like you?"

"What answers do you want that you haven't gotten from me?"

An amused smile flicked across her face. "A better question is what answers have I gotten, because that answer is zero. You've perfected the art of no comment."

"I don't think my personal life has anything to do with how I run my business."

"Maybe." Sarah took a bite. Chewed. Swallowed. "Maybe not."

"Is that what this is going to turn into? An exposé on Caleb Lewis the playboy?"

She tossed the paper wrapper into a nearby trash can and dusted off her hands. "Of course not."

Had he made the right choice when he'd gone to her desk instead of the desks of any of the other writers at *Behind the Scenes?* He tossed his trash away, then leaned against a lamppost, studying her. She had such beautiful eyes, wide and rich in color. Even behind the bronze-rimmed glasses, their unique green color showed, flashing like emeralds when she was frustrated, softening like deep jade when she was at ease. "If I trust you with this information—some of which is very sensitive proprietary information—how do I know you won't go splashing it across the gossip pages?"

"Because writing that column isn't what I really want to do."

"Then why are you doing it?"

"I was assigned to that column. I didn't ask to write it. And at the time..." She let out a sigh. "It was a job."

What had been hidden by that sigh? What piece of information had Sarah left out?

He'd started out with one image of her this morning—a get-it-at-all-costs type of reporter. Someone who wrote that drivel, and felt no compunctions about a single word. Had he been wrong? Or was she just feigning regret?

"Exactly what kind of job has you splashing my private life all over the pages of the magazine?" he asked. "And not in the most flattering manner, either."

"It wasn't a personal vendetta."

"That's what people say when they aren't the ones at the other end of the pen." Caleb paced off a couple of steps, then came back.

Damn. That had come out a lot harsher than he'd intended. He thought about explaining, then caught himself. He didn't owe anybody an explanation for his comings and goings. Certainly not the very woman who chose to post such an unflattering portrait of him.

"I'm not writing anything that isn't the truth," Sarah said, her voice low enough that only he could hear their conversation. "You *are* taking out a different model every night. You *are* seen at the hottest clubs in town until the wee hours of the morning."

"Touché." But inside…*ouch*.

Set out there like that, the truth about his life sounded so…empty. Vapid. Sarah Griffin, though, didn't know the story behind the story, and he sure as hell wasn't going to tell her now. Despite what she'd just said, he was sure she'd probably use any information he gave her about his life to move him to the top of her gossip column. It was none of her business why his social calendar was packed tighter than a jar of peanut butter.

The best thing he could do was focus the reporter's attention on something of his choosing. Like his company—instead of his nightlife.

"I'd much rather write the kind of story you've given me a taste of today. The real inside workings of a company," she said, as if she'd read his mind. "Something informative, fun and with a bit of in-depth analysis. So if you—" At this, she leaned forward, and the distance between them closed to mere inches, enough for him to inhale the light floral scent of her perfume, such a stark, fresh contrast to the overbearing floral scent of the model in the restaurant. "—want to work with me, instead of argue with me, then maybe I can put together something great. And if I do, that'll give me the perfect reason to go to my boss and get reassigned."

He'd like nothing better than to get the dogged Sarah Griffin off the subject of his personal life. Maybe some other reporter at *Behind the Scenes* would find a different fashion exec to focus the laser light of the paparazzi on.

Why had he even visited the topic of her columns? He should have just let all that alone. But that damned masochistic side of him kept insisting he should prove to Sarah Griffin that he was more than a playboy heir. Just because she was a reporter?

Or because she'd proven back in the shop that her opinion could be valuable?

Or for another reason? One that had more to do with the way she smiled and the light in her eyes?

Sarah drew the familiar slim reporter's pad out of her purse, clicked on a pen, then returned her attention to Caleb. "So, shall we?"

"Shall we what?"

"Get to work. Instead of arguing about my job."

"Getting back to work sounds like a great idea," he said. And doing that would keep him from focusing on her eyes. Her smile. The way she emphasized every point with a little flick of her hand. "As I, uh, mentioned, LL Designs is launching a shoe line this spring. If you're interested, I think it would make a great story."

"That's a press release, not a story."

"Not if you cover it from beginning to end. Design to production, as it were. I'd have you be in on every step of the process, and really see how something like this comes together."

An excited light danced in her gaze. "That would make a fabulous story. And I know the readers would love to read all that behind-the-scenes information. Not to mention it would cover one of the favorite topics at the magazine."

He chuckled. "Let me guess. Shoes?"

She quirked a grin at him. "Of course. Is there anything else more universally loved by women?"

"That's what my assistant says." He ran a hand through his hair and considered Sarah again. Maybe there could be more to this than just an interview and a little good publicity for the business.

To look at her, one wouldn't think that Sarah Griffin had any interest in fashion. She didn't wear designer clothes, didn't walk around in stilettos. Yet, just from the few comments she'd made in the factory, he knew she had an insight into the world of fashion that not everyone had. A way of looking at it, dissecting it and then offering perceptive comments.

If he spent the next few days with Sarah Griffin, allowing her that behind-the-scenes look, then he'd be taking a chance. Allowing a reporter—the very type he had always seen as the enemy—to get close, could easily backfire. But it could also be a boon. Having Sarah around would give him an opportunity to pick her brain. Not just to get her input on why LL Designs was struggling, but also maybe to find out a little more information about what his competition was up to. Why the other designers, Frederick K in particular, had managed to steal away so much of his market share. Not to mention why the other designer was suddenly so interested in buying out LL Designs.

"Are you interested in the story?"

"Very." She scribbled something on the pad. "Do you have time to talk now?"

He glanced at his watch. "I need to get back to the office, but we can talk while we walk."

She fell into step beside him, as they wove

between the people filling the sidewalk. "Tell me a little more about the company and what you're hoping to accomplish by branching out."

"My mother was...*is* a brilliant designer," Caleb began, correcting himself. Already he was making mistakes in his words. "And her designs took this company to levels I don't think even she imagined."

Sarah nodded. "LL Designs became one of the stars in the couture world. A force to be reckoned with."

"We *were*," he said, putting extra emphasis on the last word. "But then we lost our footing. Partly because my mother, uh, retired, and partly because she may have been a brilliant designer but she was a terrible businesswoman." Lenora had been the typical creative genius—scatterbrained, disorganized, frenzied about new ideas—and that had left the company in financial disarray. Everything in his mother's world, from her house to her banking records, had been a mess. Only her design books were organized and labeled so that she could instantly find everything, right down to the last scarf, in her collection. It was as if Lenora had put all her left-brain cells into that one segment of her life.

"There were rumors the company was in significant debt when she retired." Sarah jotted a few notes on the pad.

"A few months before she…left, my mother bought the building the company is in now, and had it renovated. She was counting on the next season's revenue to pick up the tab, but then she…stepped down, and things got a little rough financially. We've been working on pulling out of that, but with the economy and the decrease in couture spending, it's been an uphill battle."

"There's something I've been meaning to ask," Sarah said. Her glasses had slipped down on her nose and that inquisitive gaze connected with his.

"Shoot."

"If LL Designs is in such financial trouble, why isn't your mother here? I know she retired, but wouldn't this kind of problem draw her back, at least temporarily? To head the creative side?"

Caleb swallowed hard. He should have known this question was coming. After all, it was a logical conclusion. When the company started floundering, why not bring back its namesake and creative genius?

He considered lying, sticking to the party line he'd been spouting for more than a year. But what had that gotten him so far? Nothing but more and more entangled in a mess of his own making. Headlines blared out reporters' conjectures, most of which were wrong. At least their laser eyes weren't pointed at Lenora. Someday, though, he would have to admit the truth.

Still, he had yet to come to grips with the truth himself. How could he possibly admit it to another person?

"My mother is not planning to come back to the company, not in the near future," Caleb said.

She jotted that down. "I'm sorry," she said. "I'm sure it's hard for you without her around to ask for advice."

His gaze met hers and he wondered if it was possible he had completely misread Sarah Griffin. Maybe she wasn't the headline-seeking gossip writer who wanted only to destroy his reputation. Maybe that sigh earlier had said she was as discontented with her job as he was with the results of her coverage. Maybe they had more in common than he knew.

And that could prove just as dangerous, he realized. Because knowledge could also be a weapon, and if Sarah Griffin found out the truth about what kind of son he really was, she might just choose to use that against him.

She was a smart, witty and beautiful woman. And he'd do well to remember all of that whenever he opened his mouth.

CHAPTER FIVE

SARAH had spent three days visiting shops in and around New York with Caleb Lewis. They had stopped in boutiques, in major department stores, in salesmen's offices. In every store, with every person, she noticed one consistent fact—

Caleb Lewis was involved. Not just with the business, but with every element of it, from the designs to the distribution to the marketing. He talked to his customers, and he listened and, even more, he went back to the office with that information and implemented change. He was genuinely invested in this company, so much more than Sarah had ever thought or expected.

All this time, she'd thought he was merely a playboy who'd inherited a company he didn't really want, a figurehead blowing through the Lewis dollars with one model after another by his side.

Could she have been wrong?

Sarah sat across from Caleb Lewis in the roomy office that had once belonged to his mother, and flipped through a selection of catalogs from past seasons. For the hundredth time, she wondered why Lenora Lewis wasn't here. The woman had been so involved in her company, and then she'd just dropped out of sight. Retired, Caleb had said, and as far as Sarah had been able to determine, that was exactly what Lenora had done.

But why? Why would she walk away just as the company was floundering and leave it in the hands of her son, who was full of good intentions, but not so much experience? Why not return and give him a helping hand until the company got over this hump?

When he'd told her about his mother, Caleb had left something out, but what, she didn't know. There was definitely a detail or two, though, that he'd skipped when he was talking about Lenora and why she was no longer at the company.

Had there been a familial falling-out? A corporate disagreement? Or had Lenora been so ready to retire after forty years at the helm that she refused to return?

Whatever Caleb wasn't telling Sarah, she had the feeling it was big. Something that would make her article have that intangible element that drew in readers.

"Finding what you need?" Caleb asked.

She glanced up at him. Every time her gaze connected with his, her heart tripped. Damn. It wasn't just that Caleb was handsome, it was the way he looked at her—looked into her. "Um, yeah. Fine."

Caleb's words from the other day came back to her.

I noticed. You.

The sentences echoed in her head, and sent twin thrills of suspicion and joy running through her. Because he was buttering up the writer part of her? Or because he was genuinely interested?

She had to tread carefully. Just because a handsome man was showing her attention was no reason to lose her focus. She needed her job—needed it as much, if not more now than she ever had before.

Get back to work. Get the story, not the man.

"Have you worked up any preliminary designs for the shoe line?" she asked.

"Well, we have a few. But the problem is that we want them to complement the fall line's clothing and I'm rethinking that after your comments."

"Rethinking the fall line? But the fashion shows are only a few days away."

He ran a hand through his hair, making what had been neat a perfect mess. Sarah resisted the urge to tangle her own fingers in his dark curls. "I know. I know."

She leaned forward. "I think it's kind of like writing an article. Before I put a piece together, I figure out what tone and voice I want it to have. Snarky or serious. Funny or dramatic. If you can come up with the voice for this season's collection, then I think you'll have the direction for the new line, too."

Caleb toyed with a pencil on his desk, chewing over her words. "I've never really approached it that way before. I think so far, we've just been trying to capitalize on what has been making us successful in the past."

"Yeah, but if you ask me, what's made this company a success in the past is that it never went back. It always moved forward."

He snorted. "That's a little easier said than done."

Sarah's cell phone began to ring. The familiar chirpy tone escalated in volume, demanding an answer. Either she answered now, or he'd call back. And back. And back. Until she finally acquiesced and picked up the phone. She fished the slim phone out of her purse. "I'm sorry. I really have to take this."

Caleb nodded. "No problem."

"Hi, Dad," Sarah said into the mouthpiece. "I'm in a meeting right now and—"

"Sorry, pumpkin. But this is an emergency."

Alarm rose in Sarah. The last time he'd said that, he had cut his head open while he was getting out of the shower and needed a half dozen stitches. "Are you okay? Did you fall down?"

"Hell, no. I just can't figure out how to make this damned remote control work. Every button I push turns the TV off. I just want to watch my crime shows, not get a master's degree in techno-babble."

Sarah let out a sigh. Thank God he was okay. "Dad, something like this could have waited until I got home."

"How long is that going to take? Eight hours? Plus travel time? Do you know how long that is when I'm sitting here on this sofa of yours? Which is mighty uncomfortable, I might add. You should pick out better furniture."

Sarah bit back a gust of frustration. Her father liked to think he was being helpful when he criticized everything from her dish detergent to her oatmeal selection. Sarah had grown used to Martin's "input" long ago, and looked at it as his way of saying he loved her. Albeit, not the best way, but at least he was concerned. "Dad, let me explain the remote." She ran through the operating instructions, then said a firm goodbye and hung up the phone. "Sorry about that," she said to Caleb.

"I understand. I worked for my mother off and on through high school and college. It was... challenging sometimes. We loved each other, but there were days when we drove each other nuts." With that, another small thread extended between them, knitted from shared experiences. She shrugged it off. The last thing she needed was a connection with this man. For one, she didn't have time, and for another—

She clearly wasn't his type. Hadn't she gotten that message in the restaurant the other day? Or when some of the models had paraded by his office earlier this morning and "popped in" just to say hi to Caleb—spending a good ten minutes flirting with him?

Beautiful, leggy women, with the kind of looks Sarah had always wanted, but somehow never mastered. Not that she'd spent a whole lot of time trying. She'd been too busy holding her family together and holding down a job to do much more than apply lipstick in the morning. She hadn't thought much about her lack of morning prep until now, when it seemed the entire fashion world was strutting by her table, and attracting the attention of the man across from her.

What if she did look like one of those women? Would Caleb Lewis brush his lips across her cheeks? Would he flash her that smile of his? Ask her on a date?

Insane thoughts, Sarah. Buy a tube of mascara and get over the whole fantasizing-about-Caleb Lewis thing.

She cleared her throat. "Now, to get back to what you were about to—"

The phone started again. The same peppy tone that was hooked to one specific caller—

Her father.

"Dad," she hissed into the phone. "I'm in a meeting. I can't talk right now."

"I know, I know, and I'm sorry, but this will only take a second."

Sarah rubbed her temples. "Okay. What?"

"I was trying to be helpful, you know, and so I started making something to eat, and well…" He paused a second. "I had a mishap."

Oh, this didn't bode well. At all. The last time her father had helped cook, she'd had to call the fire department. "Dad, step away from the stove. I'll be home soon."

She rose, stuffing her phone back in her purse. "I'm extremely sorry, but I really have to go."

"Parental troubles?" Caleb came around his desk and stood before her.

Sarah sighed. "You have no idea. My father moved in with me last year and he's been...difficult. He means well, but he's not exactly Mr. Self-Sufficient. Sometimes, I feel like I have a toddler at home."

"Want a hand with that?" Caleb reached for her before she stepped away. The momentary contact seared her skin.

She eyed him. "Why would you want to help me?"

"Because I know what it's like to be a parental babysitter of sorts, and maybe I can run interference for you."

The thought of having someone else there to help her get through to her stubborn father sounded good. Very good. Just someone else to shoulder the burdens that Sarah had been carrying way too long by herself.

But Caleb Lewis? Oh, that could be a dangerous mistake. Mixing business with personal? Hadn't she vowed a thousand times to keep things between them strictly professional? Not to get caught up in his touch, his eyes, his smile? For the past few days, she'd done a good job of keeping things on a business-only level. They'd talked about the company, toured shops, spent time in the factory. All the while, she'd been aware of him—she couldn't get within five feet of the man and not be overwhelmingly aware of him—but she hadn't acted on any of those feelings.

And now she was considering bringing him home to meet her father? If anything opened the door to a relationship, that did.

"I shouldn't…"

"You should," Caleb said, placing a hand on her arm again. Zings ran through her, and she told herself to pull away. Told herself to break the contact.

She did neither.

"I can see the stress all over your face," he said. "And take it from someone who has been there. A helping hand, even if it's just to negotiate dinner prep, can make all the difference in the world."

Oh, having Caleb Lewis spend more time with her was going to make a difference. That, she could tell just by the way her traitorous hormones ran through in a frenzy. But that kind of difference could be dangerous.

A huge step out of her comfort zone.

Wasn't that what she was supposed to be doing? Part of the whole new life plan? Nevertheless, she hadn't done a single out-of-the-comfort-zone thing except take home those Frederick Ks without her boss's knowledge or permission. Look how well that had turned out.

Sarah glanced at Caleb. "Maybe—"

Then yet another model poked her head into his office, calling out Caleb's name. Sarah drew herself up. This was *Caleb Lewis*. The man who personified playboy. He was a lot more trouble than a pair of stilettos.

"Thanks," she said, offering him a smile, "but I'm just fine on my own. Good day, Mr. Lewis."

Night fell, draping its blanket of darkness over the city. Outside, streetlights flickered on, incandescent bulbs warmed homes and hearths and people settled in for the end of the day.

But not Caleb Lewis. He sat in his apartment, watching the city blink outside his window. From here, it seemed like hundreds of fireflies flicking their glowing tails, flitting into a window, along a walkway, down a busy street. Jazz music played on his stereo, a lonely sweet melody filling the dark corners of the apartment, dancing life over the inanimate furniture.

He sipped at a bourbon on the rocks. The pricey liquor slid down his throat with a slight satiny burn. The alcohol didn't make anything easier, but it sure as hell made it seem as if he could sit here long enough and the right decision would just come to him. Dozens of nights he'd spent sitting in this chair, sometimes even falling asleep where he sat, and he had yet to figure out a damned thing.

There was a gentle nudge at his elbow. Caleb glanced down. "Hey, Mac. I bet I know what you want."

The chocolate lab panted out a yes-yes, then, when Caleb didn't get to his feet, the seven-year-old dog let out a sigh and dropped to his haunches beside Caleb's chair. Patient, quiet. Knowing his master would eventually pull himself out of this funk, snap on the leash and take both of them out into the night. Or even better, fill the food bowl with a second meal of the day.

Caleb rubbed the dog's head, and Mac pressed himself against the chair. The dog, so loyal and, yet, so unaware of the agonizing decisions racing through Caleb's head. How he tossed around the same list of pros and cons and impossible solutions. "What would you do?"

The dog didn't answer. He never did. If Caleb really wanted an answer, he'd ask a human.

Instead, he sipped at the bourbon and watched the city. And thought about where he had gone wrong in his life, and how he would probably try to fill that hole again tonight with yet another loud, mindless night.

And in the end, come back here, exhausted,

but no more fulfilled. No happier than when he'd left and certainly no closer to the right decision.

Or...he could make another choice. One that sent him down a different path than the crooked one he'd been following for way too long.

"What are you, some kind of stalker?" Martin Griffin crossed his arms over his chest and eyed Caleb. He was a tall man with a barrel chest—at least six inches taller than Caleb—and he used that height advantage to loom large and imposing.

Caleb had seen the badge encased in glass on the mantel and wondered if the interrogation was because Martin was a former cop or because he was a father or both. Either way, Caleb couldn't blame the man. If Sarah had been his daughter he'd have been suspicious of any man showing up on the doorstep.

For the fourth time since he'd rung Sarah Griffin's doorbell, Caleb wondered if he'd done the wrong thing. He'd gotten her address out of the phone book, and just shown up on her doorstep. Instead of finding Sarah at the door though, he found her father.

"Uh, no, sir. Not a stalker at all," Caleb said.

"Just making sure." Martin leaned in closer

His light blue eyes seemed to see into Caleb's brain and the scowl on his face said he wasn't happy with what he was reading there. "You never know when some stranger follows my little girl home."

"I didn't follow her. I just stopped by to visit."

Martin harrumphed. Showing how much he believed that.

The apartment door opened and Sarah breezed in, a large tote bag stuffed with papers slung over her shoulder. Clearly, she'd just left work, and like him, brought as much of it home as she left behind in the office. "Hey, Dad, I was thinking for dinner we could—"

The sentence died in her throat when she saw Caleb. "What are you doing here?"

"I offered to help, remember?"

"You want me to get rid of him?" Martin asked, staring at Caleb as though he was a trash bag, ready to be hauled to the curb. "Is he one of those crazy guys who can't take no for an answer?"

"No, not at all. Caleb is a…" Her voice trailed off and she glanced at him.

"Colleague," Caleb finished.

Could he have picked a lamer description? But another option didn't come to mind. He and

Sarah weren't friends, exactly, and they certainly weren't lovers. They were...

Colleagues, as cold as that word sounded. Distant. And not at all the kind of thoughts he'd been having this whole week. They'd spent day after day together, and though their every conversation had been about work, his mind had been elsewhere. Fantasizing about kissing her, about taking her in his arms, and about what it would feel like to run his hand over that sweet peach skin—that didn't fit in the description of work peers.

Yeah, probably not the best thing to tell her father.

Martin harrumphed again, then crossed the room and dropped into a leather recliner that had seen better days. Its battered brown sides and duct-tape-repaired footrest stood in stark contrast to the sleek white-and-glass modern furniture filling the rest of the room, furnishings that reflected Sarah's fresh, direct personality. Clearly, the chair had come with Martin.

Sarah sighed and rolled her eyes at her father before turning to Caleb. "Can I get you something to drink?" she said to Caleb.

"Get the man a beer," Martin said before Caleb could answer. "Men like beer."

Caleb grinned. "Beer's fine."

She ducked into the kitchen, leaving Caleb

alone with her father. Martin eyed him as if he might make off with the silver at any moment. Clearly, Caleb wasn't racking up too many brownie points here.

"What do you want for dinner, Dad?" Sarah called from the kitchen. "I have some chicken in the fridge—"

"Not anymore." Martin frowned. "That damned stove gets too hot. My chicken fricassee got fricasseed and then some."

Sarah returned, handing an opened beer to Caleb. "Okay, then the steaks I bought. Those—"

"Have gone on to a better place." Martin put up his hands in a wasn't-my-fault gesture. "That broiler ain't much better."

"Didn't I tell you to shut off the stove today?"

"I did. After I tried cooking a meal." Martin scowled. "I was trying to be helpful, you know." His face softened. "You do too much for me, little girl, and I was just trying to repay you a little."

"I know. And I appreciate it, but really, Dad, I don't mind cooking." Sarah crossed to the closet, and hung up her coat, then did the same with Caleb's. "How about I just open a can of soup? You like that tomato one."

"Or I could take you all out," Caleb cut in.

He could read the frustration bubbling in Sarah from across the room. Undoubtedly, this kitchen-disaster scenario had played out more than once before between father and daughter.

Martin kicked out the base of the recliner, then clicked on the television. A game show roared to life. "I don't like going out. Too much work involved just to get a meal."

Sarah sighed. "Dad—"

"Then we'll order in. No work for anyone." Caleb flipped out his cell phone. "What would you like, Martin? Steak? Burgers?"

There was a pause as Martin assessed Caleb. "Well, if you're going to force me to eat..." A ghost of a smile appeared on Martin's face. "Steak. Medium. Baked potato with all the extras. And lots of rolls."

"Dad, there's hardly a vegetable in that."

Martin shrugged. "Potato's a vegetable."

"All health benefits are canceled by the sour cream, the butter, the salt and the bacon bits you put on top of it." Sarah made a face. "Not to mention all the white flour in the—"

"Sarah, you know I love you. And I know you love me, too. But if you try to tell me about one more thing that's going to clog my arteries or raise my cholesterol, I think I'll have to ground you."

Sarah laughed. "I am far too old to be

grounded. And someone needs to tell you how to take care of yourself. God knows you're not going to do it. The doctor has already told you to watch your meat consumption. If you'd just have more vegetables, you'd be a lot healthier."

"Vegetables, shmegetables." Martin patted his ample belly. "I'm a meat-and-potatoes guy. Always will be. You aren't going to change that."

Sarah ceded the argument and sent Caleb a smile of gratitude. The best she could do was sneak some vegetables into the spaghetti sauce, add pureed apples to her father's morning oatmeal, and insist he take a vitamin every day. Martin Griffin had always been a stubborn man, and Sarah had learned to pick her battles. She needed to accept she wasn't going to win the one over vegetables.

Caleb shot her a grin, then completed his call, placing the order for delivery. While they waited for the food, Caleb and her father exchanged small talk and Sarah set about cleaning up the disaster in her kitchen from her father's attempt at chicken fricassee. She soaked the burner covers, expended about a thousand calories scrubbing off the burnt bits of food in the oven and the cooktop, then did dishes until her fingers wrinkled.

By the time she came out of the kitchen, Caleb

and Martin were chatting and laughing like old friends. She paused in the entryway, watching them. She hadn't seen her father smile that much in years. His face was animated, his eyes bright, and the laughter that poured from him was the deep, hearty sound she had missed so much over the last few years.

Her dad—like he used to be, before his wife died and his world turned inside-out. Ever since then, he'd been a ghost of himself. She'd tried everything—calling his old friends, insisting he join a book club, dragging him to nearly every new movie released, but nothing had worked. Until now.

The change she had prayed to see in him was finally coming to light. Tears sprang to her eyes, but she whisked them away before they made an appearance on her cheeks.

The doorbell rang. Caleb answered it and insisted on paying for dinner, even though Sarah offered several times. "My treat," he said.

"Thank you. You really don't have to do all this."

He laughed. "Ah, but isn't this my specialty?"

"What?"

"Sharing a meal with a beautiful woman."

Beautiful. She tried not to let the word affect her. To tell herself he was just joking. She was so far from his type, she wasn't on the same planet.

And besides, she knew what kind of man he was. She'd written the sentences that described him as a "footloose bachelor," a "determined playboy," a "charming heir to the fashion throne."

But the man she saw in her apartment living room, the one who had eased the tension between her and her father, who had gotten Martin to laugh and smile, didn't seem to fit any of those adjectives. Was it all an act just to get her to write more positive stories about him? Or was this man the true Caleb, the one who existed under the intoxicating smile and models hanging on his every word?

"Thank you," she said, taking the food from him. Their fingertips brushed and a heat that had nothing to do with the food raced along Sarah's skin. She had gone all these days without touching him, but the thought of what his touch would be like had always been there in the back of her mind.

"Anytime," Caleb said.

Sarah just nodded and headed back into the kitchen. *Don't think about him. Don't give in to the temptation.*

She busied herself with dishing up the food and setting the kitchen table. A few minutes later, the three of them sat around her small round walnut table. Despite everything she'd just vowed, she couldn't help but notice how domestic it all felt. Sitting across from Caleb gave her an image of the future.

If only.

If only he wasn't who he was. If only she would take a chance on him. If only she believed in fairy tales instead of writing about the dissolution of happily-ever-afters.

"Wherever you got this food from," Sarah said, "it's delicious."

"I agree," Martin said as he finished off his last bite of steak. "Best damned cow I've ever eaten."

Caleb smiled. "You really liked it?"

Martin gestured at the half a steak remaining on Caleb's plate. "You gonna eat that, skinny? Because if you aren't, I will."

Caleb pushed his plate across the table. "Help yourself."

Her father polished off his second helpings in record time. Then he sat back in his chair and rubbed a circle over his stomach. "If I had known a kitchen disaster would bring about a meal like that, I'd have set the stove on fire a long time ago."

"Dad! I hope you're not serious."

Her father sent her a wink.

"I'd be glad to treat you again," Caleb said. "Especially to a meal so good for your health."

Martin chuckled. "Good for my health. That's a good one."

"I'm serious." Caleb leaned in, and caught Sarah's gaze for a moment. "Because this 'steak' dinner was actually vegetarian. Soy steak, as it were."

Martin jerked back, as if the plate might bite him. His silverware clattered onto the white porcelain. "Soy? As in that bean thing?"

"Yep. Tastes just like the real thing, doesn't it?"

"Well…yeah, it does. Tastes damned good, in fact." Martin glanced back down at his empty plate and chuckled. "Well, I'll be. Fake steak. Ain't that the damndest thing ever?" He rose, and clapped a hand on Caleb's shoulder. "I like this one, Sarah. Bring him around again."

Then her father headed back into the living room to catch a rerun of his favorite sitcom, still puzzling over the dinner switch while Sarah and Caleb cleaned up. She loaded the dishes into soapy water and he bundled up the few leftovers into plastic containers. Sarah turned the water off, then pivoted and put her back to the sink. "Thank you."

"You're welcome." He grinned again, and she realized she was getting used to seeing his smile. One of these days—soon—she'd be done with the article and she'd only see that smile when he used it on another woman in a nightclub.

That day wasn't today. Thank goodness.

"You did a great thing today. It was more than just the steak." She smiled. "Where did you get the idea to order vegetarian steak?"

"My mother. She also had high cholesterol and blood pressure that made the nurse cringe. Didn't matter to my mother. She liked what she liked, and that was it, no arguments. She was going to have her chocolate cake and the sauce on the side, too." A smile flitted across his face, but this one was bittersweet. What secrets did he keep tucked in that gesture? "So I called around to all the bakeries in the area until I found one that made a healthy chocolate cake. She couldn't tell the difference, and after that, as long as it tasted like the real thing, she'd eat it."

"I went through the same things with my mother," Sarah said. She plunged the sponge into a glass, then rinsed it, and paused a moment before putting it in the strainer. "When I was ten, my mother got breast cancer. She beat it the first time, but then it came back, and she had a long, long tough time before she died. I did my best to make her healthy meals that tasted good but sometimes getting her to eat was a battle."

Caleb's hand lighted on her shoulder. "I'm sorry. That must have been so hard on you."

She nodded, and felt the sting of tears against the back of her eyes. Oh, damn. She didn't want to cry. Not now. Not in front of Caleb.

His hand lingered on her, and a tear slid down Sarah's cheek. "I'm sorry."

"Don't apologize. How long ago did she die?"

Sarah's gaze met his. "Two years. Some days it feels like yesterday."

"I'm sorry," he said again, and she could hear the heartfelt sentiment in his voice, the sympathy in the syllables.

She nodded, then sighed, and put the glass in the strainer before reaching for another. "Have you ever watched someone you love go through something so painful, so difficult, you find yourself praying for their suffering to end?"

There was a long pause, so long, Sarah glanced over at Caleb. His features were as set as stone, his gaze on something outside her window. "No. But I can imagine how difficult it must be."

She had a feeling there was something more he wanted to say. She waited, the dishes simply soaking. Whatever it was, Caleb didn't say anything more. Instead, he held up a platter. "Uh, where does this go?"

"In the cabinet in the hall."

He disappeared to put the dish away, and probably to put an end to a difficult conversation. She regretted bringing up her mother. She'd opened a door to her personal life that she had kept shut for years—and to the last person in the world she would have thought she'd open it to. But there'd just been something about Caleb, something that seemed to say that he understood.

Why him, of all people?

He returned to the kitchen, picked up the towel and waited for her to wash more dishes. "Your dad really seemed to enjoy dinner tonight."

Subject of her mother definitely closed. Good.

"He did." Sarah deposited a clean plate into the strainer. "You'll have to give me the name of that restaurant. Maybe I should set up a standing order."

Caleb pulled the damp plate out of the strainer and swiped it with a dish towel. "Sure. No problem." He held up the plate, a question on his face, and she gestured toward the cabinet on his left. Caleb slipped the plate inside, then reached for another.

As he did, he came within a millimeter of touching her. Every fiber inside her was acutely aware of the nearness of him. The way his T-shirt hugged his muscular frame, outlining a body that had clearly spent a lot of time in the gym. As she watched him handle the dishes, a part of her wondered if he would handle her with that same care and attention to detail.

The connection that had formed between them all those days ago had deepened tonight, augmented by the way he had taken care of her father, how he had stepped in with a simple phone call, a few words. Who knew a takeout order could change things so much?

"You know, I'm not as evil as you like to think I am." His words broke the silence.

"I never said you were evil." She concentrated on making concentric circles with the sponge, watching the soap bubbles multiply, disappear, multiply again.

"You might have thought it a time or ten when you were writing about me. Admit it."

A laugh escaped her. "Okay, maybe. But not evil, more…devilish."

"I assure you, I'm neither. What you see and what's reality are two different things."

She let the silverware in her hands slip back to the bottom of the sink, then turned toward him. "Oh, really? Then who are you, Caleb Lewis?"

He put down the dish towel and moved closer to her, so close, all she had to do was take a step, maybe two, and she'd be in his arms. Her heart rate accelerated, her pulse thundered in her veins.

"I'm just an ordinary man trying to run a company. One who doesn't know what the hell he's doing most days, but who keeps showing up anyway."

"Good." Anything with more than one syllable seemed impossible to say.

"Yeah," he said, his voice soft, quiet. Sexy.

Her breath caught and held, every ounce of her captured by his blue eyes. Caleb leaned in closer, propping one hand on the edge of the sink, nearly touching her waist. Electricity hummed inside her.

"I'm really a very nice guy." He was so close, he could have kissed her without any effort at all. She wanted him to––oh, how she wanted him to kiss her. Wanted to feel his lips against hers, to taste him, hold him. To see if the reality was anywhere near as good as the fantasy.

"I believe that," she said, the words almost a whisper.

"Do you?"

"After tonight, yes, I do."

A smile quirked up one side of his face. "Good."

"Then what's a nice guy like you doing out on the town almost every night?"

The wall between them couldn't have been rebuilt faster if a team of masons had come in to lay the cement. Caleb backed up, grabbed the dish towel again, then withdrew another plate from the strainer. "That's different. It's….hard to explain."

"Why don't you try?" Which Caleb was he? She still didn't know. There were parts of Caleb Lewis that he kept to himself, parts that were partitioned off from her, from the rest of the world. Why?

He held up the plate. "Where does this go again?"

"Same place as all the others." She gestured to the cabinet on his left. "Are you avoiding the question?"

"I just don't think it's pertinent."

"To what?"

"To the piece you want to do on the company. I am not the company, nor is my social life. I'm sure you can write a fair, balanced and incisive piece, without including what martini I ordered at the 21 Club last week."

"Of course I can." Sarah pulled the plug, watching the water drain away. She should be glad there was distance between them again. Glad she'd avoided being kissed by one of the most well-known playboys in New York. This was what she wanted, wasn't it?

Of course. Except for that part of her that already missed Caleb's grin.

"I need to get going," Caleb said. "Early day tomorrow."

Back to work. Which was where her mind should be going, too. "About the shoe..." In the last few days, she'd nearly forgotten all about it, but she knew Karl would be back to work tomorrow, which meant she had to have the Frederick K back, too.

"Can you come by my office first thing tomorrow? I'll give you that and we can finish up whatever else you need for the article." Caleb hung the towel on the oven-door handle. The move seemed so final, and despite her better judgment, a part of Sarah wanted to ask him to stay. To ease this constant ache in her body for more...for him.

One night wouldn't make any difference one way or the other, Sarah decided. And a few hours away from Caleb would surely help her clear her head. "Of course."

The grin curved across his face, and something deep inside Sarah fluttered. "I look forward to it."

She did, too. The problem was how much.

Sarah saw Caleb to the door. On the way, he stopped to say goodbye to her father. His gaze swept over her apartment, and he was seeing, no doubt, how different she was from all the other women he knew. She would be smart to remember that and stick to what she did best.

Write the story and stay uninvolved with the subject.

CHAPTER SIX

PEDRO had sent Sarah a half a dozen texts before she even got out the door, warning her that Karl was on the warpath about the Frederick K shoes, wondering where they were and if both they and Sarah had skipped town. "He sez U better B in the Witness Protection program or B dead," Pedro texted. "Did U find Prince Charming yet?"

Oh, she'd found a prince all right. The prince at the head of LL Designs. And he was definitely charming. But as for being the right prince for this Cinderella—

All she wanted from him was the shoe, not the ride into the sunset on the back of a white stallion.

Except her hormones didn't seem to be getting the message. After Caleb had left the night before, Sarah had lain awake for hours, replaying those moments in the kitchen. What if he *had* kissed her? What would she have done?

Pushed him away—or drawn him closer still? "You can go in now."

Sarah jerked to attention. "Oh. Thank you."

The gray-haired woman at the assistant's desk nodded and went back to typing entries into the scheduling program open on her computer. Clearly, she was Caleb's assistant and chief guard dog, judging by the way she'd fended off employees stopping by and the unending phone calls.

Sarah squared her shoulders, then strode into Caleb's office. Regardless of yesterday, and that moment of weakness in her kitchen, she refused to let him affect her today. She was here for business reasons. Nothing else.

He stood by the window, his tall, lean frame silhouetted by the bright sun. A stunning view of the city painted in the spaces around Caleb, but Sarah's gaze remained on the man. He had a tension to his stance. A set to his jaw. And when he turned to face her, she saw a flicker of melancholy in his blue gaze.

She opened her mouth, about to ask what was wrong, then shut it again.

How did she know for sure he wasn't just using her, like so many others she had met, to drum up publicity? What if his interest was merely a guise? How many heartbreaks had she witnessed, just by covering the incestuous revolving world of fashion? Models dumped for aspiring actresses, aging CEOs trading in wives for girls barely out of college.

Starry-eyed reporters left in the dust by narcissistic designers who used the people around them for PR. She had to be honest with herself. She wasn't a model. She wasn't devastatingly beautiful. She was just Sarah. An ordinary girl with ordinary looks and an ordinary job. Nothing glamorous in this package, nothing like the kind of woman she normally saw on Caleb's arm. And that meant there was a distinct possibility that was all Caleb wanted, even though a part of her wanted to believe otherwise. Wanted to read more into that moment by a sudsy sink.

"Sarah." A smile curved across Caleb's face, and every protest in Sarah's mind flitted away.

His smile was intoxicating.

"I realize you probably have a busy day ahead of you," Sarah said, reminding herself to *focus,* "so I won't take up too much of your time. In fact, I think I have about everything I need for my article, so if you have—"

"It's fine. I was looking forward to your visit today." He gestured toward the visitor chair across from his desk. He slipped in behind the massive cherry piece, then pulled open a drawer. "I believe this is yours." He set the Frederick K stiletto before her.

She'd brought the mate from home, intending to go to the office as soon as she left LL Designs. Sarah wrangled the left one from her purse, then sat it beside the right. It seemed as if both shoes brightened once they were paired again. Alone, one shoe had been pretty. Interesting. But together, the two together screamed sexiness, allure. Sarah reached out and ran a finger down the slim T-strap, her fingers skipping over the delicate stitching, the gold buckle ornamentation at the crux of the T. She skimmed over the arch, then down the heel. She'd seen hundreds of pairs of shoes in her years at the fashion magazine, but these ones seemed to embody the woman she wished she'd had a chance to be.

"They're beautiful, aren't they?" she said.

"They are. Frederick K might not be the kind of guy I'd want to share a beer with, but I have to admit he is brilliant at his job."

"It's like he read my mind and produced the perfect shoe. Exactly what I was dreaming of buying." She'd spent her life being practical, being the responsible one. She worked, she took care of her family and she worried. Stilettos didn't fit in that equation.

"Then why aren't you wearing yours?"

"What are you talking about? These ones aren't even for sale."

"I saw the shoes at your apartment yesterday."

The closet door, the one in the hall by the cabinet where Caleb had put away the serving dish. She'd forgotten that it had been ajar. She rarely closed it, because she rarely had company. "You saw my collection."

"Gathering dust, I assume."

"I just don't get occasions to wear them."

"Why not?" Caleb leaned over his desk, and with the movement, she caught the notes of his cologne. The subtle woodsy scent, chased by spice.

"It's complicated." She sighed. "I'm...practical. I buy those shoes on impulse, but I never wear them. They don't fit into my world."

"You work in the fashion industry—doesn't wearing high heels go along with the job description?"

"Aren't you quite the question man today? Why are you suddenly so interested in my footwear selection?"

Caleb wove his hands together and put them on the desk. "Let's call it research."

She wasn't sure she believed him a hundred percent, but decided to play along anyway. After all, he'd been answering her questions all week. The least she could do is answer a few of his. "All my life, I've done the responsible thing.

Paid my bills on time, balanced my checkbook, put in the hours at work. And yes, every once in a while, I go a little crazy and buy a pair of shoes like this, but Lord only knows why, because…" She hesitated, then finished the sentence. "…I don't have any place to wear them."

There. The truth was out. Sarah Griffin had the social life of a turtle. The only time she went to a hot, hip spot, it was to work. Not on a date, not out with friends.

"Well then, we'll just have to do something about that, won't we?" Caleb said.

Sarah couldn't read the look on his face. Was he asking her out? Or merely making a comment? "I'm not so sure it would be a good idea for the gossip reporter to be seen out on the town with the subject of her gossip column."

"Except you aren't writing that column right this second, since you're doing the articles instead. So it's not really a conflict of interest, is it?"

He had a point. Still…going out with Caleb Lewis would only bring them closer together, and given the way her thoughts refused to leave the kiss-me-now path, that probably wouldn't be a good idea. She glanced again at the Frederick Ks. "These shoes are the epitome of impractical. They're like the poster shoes for reckless living."

"True," Caleb said. "Either way, they'd look amazing on you."

Sarah jerked her hand away from the stilettos. "Oh, I can't wear these. I'm supposed to be writing about them, not putting them on."

"What size are you?"

"Seven, but—"

"That's what these are." Caleb nudged the shoes closer to her. "Try them on."

"Oh, no, I shouldn't—"

"You should." He grinned, and in that moment, she couldn't tell which was more tempting—the forbidden shoes or the forbidden man. "Indulge, Sarah."

For a second, she wondered about indulging in Caleb Lewis. In his lips, his touch, letting herself fall into the deep tones of his voice. Finish what they had started in her kitchen last night, fulfill the fantasies that had filled her dreams after she'd gone to bed. Because something had definitely started by her sink yesterday—and ended much too quickly. "In-indulge?"

He rose, and came around his desk, then picked up one of the shoes and dropped to the space beside her chair. "Shall I?"

With him right there, his smile cemented on his face, and his blue gaze locked on hers, anything other than assent seemed impossible. She put out her foot, and nodded. "Please do."

Who was this woman? Sarah Griffin didn't get swept up by charming men. Sarah Griffin didn't live life as Cinderella. Sarah Griffin was practical, resolved and focused.

But that Sarah Griffin seemed a hundred miles away as Caleb reached over, slid off the sensible black boots that were her everyday shoes, and replaced them with the Frederick K stilettos. His hand brushed against her instep, and a shiver chased through her.

Oh, this was bad. So bad. Not just wearing the shoes but the way she reacted to him, her hormones clamoring for more. More touches, more smiles and just…more in general.

"Beautiful, like I said." Caleb rocked back on his heels and gestured at her feet.

Sarah glanced down and saw the same feet she'd had her entire life, but transformed somehow into sleek, elegant, sexy appendages. The shoes' soft leather caressed her skin, begged to be worn, walked in. Suddenly everything about her that had felt dowdy this morning— the jeans, the sweater, her hair down and un-adorned—seemed to disappear, as if she hadn't just changed her shoes, but had also changed every ounce of her appearance. She felt beautiful. Desirable. Confident. Sarah rose and before she could think about the wisdom of what she was about to do—

She walked across the room. Goodness, she even carried herself differently. Her hips held a sway they never had before and her chest seemed to thrust forward on its own. "It's like walking on clouds. Really, really high clouds."

Caleb chuckled. Then he crossed to her. "That's the look I want to see."

Her breath caught. "You do?"

He nodded, and his smile seemed to hold her captive. "Perfect."

"Thank you." The words escaped her on a breath. What were they talking about? And did she really care anyway?

Caleb caught her jaw in his palm and cradled her gently. His thumb traced the corner of her smile. The added height of the shoes brought her gaze even with his blue one, and brought her mouth right to his. "Sarah..."

Her name was a whisper between them, and for the first time in her life, Sarah realized the intoxicating power of having a man's full attention on her. She'd dated, yes, but always in a sort of distracted way, with her mind back on the millions of things waiting for her at home. The people who counted on her, who needed her. Never had she had the freedom, the luxury, to just enjoy a man's attention.

Her body swayed, and the distance between them closed from inches to centimeters. Sarah's gaze dropped to Caleb's lips. Desire surged inside her.

Kiss me.

The need for his touch arced in her body. She was a hundred times more aware of him than she ever had been before. Aware of every beat of her heart, every breath that escaped her. Was it the shoes? Was it the way they had made her aware of herself as a woman?

She didn't care. She wanted him. *Now*.

Instead of waiting for Caleb, this new Sarah, the one who had been emboldened by a pair of sexy shoes and simply couldn't stay in the shadows anymore, leaned in toward him, and brushed her lips against his. His eyes widened in surprise, but then he cupped her head, and drew her in even more. His lips drifted over hers, but she didn't want a simple, quiet kiss.

She wanted more.

She wanted it all.

She grabbed his back and pressed him to her, then opened her mouth against his. Her tongue danced across his lips, and when he opened and yielded to the touch, she tasted him, teasing his tongue with hers.

Caleb groaned, heat exploding between them as the kiss deepened. He didn't just kiss her—he captured her mouth with a magic that set off fireworks inside her, that awakened parts of her body she hadn't even been aware were slumbering. She moved closer to him, the hard solidness of his chest meeting her soft curves with a protective strength. Her hands roamed up and down his back, slipping over the muscles rippling beneath the cotton fabric of his shirt.

He pulled back, but didn't release her. Her heart kept on racing, as if it were an engine that refused to slow. "Well," Caleb said, his grin extending to his eyes. "I didn't expect that."

"Neither did I."

What had she been thinking?

She hadn't been, that was clear. But right now, she didn't care. She moved closer again, hoping to pick up where they'd left off. Finish that kiss and begin another, for one.

"I, uh, was going to say that your reaction to wearing those shoes was exactly the kind of reaction I want to see in the faces of the women who wear LL Designs." Caleb's words poured an ice bath on her senses. She stepped back, the desire that had been a fire in her earlier cooling. "But, ah, then you took it a step further than I was picturing."

Oh, damn. He'd been talking business, and she'd thought he was talking attraction. What a fool she had been. All along this had been about business, not a relationship.

Sarah stumbled back, nearly toppling in the

five-inch heels. What a fool she had been. What a colossal mistake she'd made. "I'm sorry. I should have..." She couldn't find words to explain what had just happened. All she wanted to do was get out of there.

She didn't care about the article. Didn't care about the deal she'd made with Caleb Lewis. She turned, grabbed her purse from the floor, and ran out of his office before she could be tempted any further.

Caleb was halfway out of his office when he stopped himself. He should let her go. He had no business getting involved with Sarah Griffin. Or anyone, for that matter.

But particularly not with a woman like Sarah. She wasn't one of the flighty models who pursued him as though he was the lone chocolate bar at an all-vegetable buffet. She wasn't one of the hundreds of women he'd met who were interested only in what he could do for their careers.

No, Sarah Griffin was a strong, independent woman. One who offered the kind of challenge that intrigued Caleb, drew him in like a spider to a fly. Made him want to touch her, kiss her, talk to her.

And she was also the woman who held the power in her hands to completely destroy his reputation and by extension, that of LL Designs. He needed to keep that in mind rather than allowing himself to get lost in those green eyes and that sassy mouth. A mouth that had tasted like honey. Felt like satin beneath his.

Damn. Already he wanted her again. Wanted to see where that kiss would have led if he hadn't tried to be a gentleman. Not that he'd been so smooth about that, what with his idiotic comment about how he wanted his customers to react to his shoe line.

Moron.

All he'd been thinking about was bringing the heat between them to a halt before things got out of hand.

Out of hand—

With Sarah Griffin, Caleb suspected that would be an adventure to remember.

"What the hell just happened?" Martha waved toward the elevator doors. "I've never seen a woman leave your office that fast before."

"Gee, thanks."

"Sorry, boss." Martha spun in her chair until she was facing him. Over the year that Caleb had been in charge of the company, his mother's former assistant had gone from being a right-hand help to being a mentor of sorts. She bridged the old world and the new, and had no compunctions about telling him where he was going wrong. "So what was her problem with you anyway?"

"I kissed her," Caleb said.

"You...you kissed Sarah Griffin?" Martha's jaw dropped. "Why?"

Caleb chuckled. "Well, I think the why is obvious. She's an intriguing, beautiful woman. And technically...she kissed me first."

"She kissed you?" Disbelief tinted every word. "You?"

"Am I that much of an ogre?"

Martha laughed. "No, not at all. Just...I thought she hated you."

"I did, too." But in the last couple of days that they had been together, Caleb had realized that the layers of his relationship with Sarah Griffin, if one could call their interactions a relationship, were complicated. She wasn't the evil gossip writer he'd painted her to be. She wasn't vindictive or cruel.

She was honest.

And if he sat back and looked at those articles, ignoring the exclamation points and the oversized headlines, he knew he'd get a story about his life. One he didn't want to read.

"I need to get back to work," he said.

Martha wagged a finger at him. "No. You need to go talk to that girl."

"Are you kidding me? She's probably back

at her office, writing up two pages on how the lonely CEO seduced her."

Martha laughed. "You said *she* kissed *you.* I'd say those tables were turned."

And they had been—in a way that had surprised, and, yes, delighted him. He'd never expected take-no-guff Sarah Griffin to make the first move. "True. Still, it's better if I stick to work. The company—"

"Won't go bankrupt in the next hour. Haven't you ever heard the old adage?"

"What adage is that?"

"If the CEO ain't happy, ain't nobody happy. And you, Caleb, aren't happy. At all." Her face softened. "You haven't been in a long, long time."

"I don't need to date a reporter to be happy." Especially not that one. If he got involved with Sarah, he'd be mixing business and pleasure, and that could only lead to disaster.

Who was he kidding? He was already involved. More than he wanted to be, more than he'd imagined being. And yet he couldn't seem to untangle himself from the web with Sarah Griffin.

Martha shook her head. "I disagree. That woman could be the one."

"No matter how intriguing she is, she's still the gossip reporter at the magazine."

"True. Though I think that kiss is a sign that you're changing her mind about the kind of man she thinks you are." Martha leaned forward, and her kind light-blue eyes met his. "I already know the truth, and I think it's about time the world does, too."

Caleb scowled. "I don't need to splash my private life onto the pages of a fashion magazine."

"Oh, Caleb," Martha said, sympathy coating her tone, "what makes you think the media would be such a harsh judge?"

Because he had already judged and convicted himself of his actions in his mind. Guilty of abandonment. Guilty of being too consumed by his own life to be there when he was needed most.

If only he'd come in earlier that day. If only he'd been more of a partner to his mother, as she'd asked. He would have been there in her office when the stroke hit early that Tuesday morning, and he would have called the ambulance within that golden hour.

Instead, she'd waited. Suffering. Caleb completely unaware of what was happening just a few blocks away. Out for brunch with a date instead of sitting on the other side of his mother's desk.

All he'd done ever since was try to make it

up to her. Try to prove that he did care, that she could trust him with her company. Thus far, he'd done a lousy job.

Martha was the only one who knew the truth about the decisions he had made and the ones he had yet to make. Why she still sang his praises, Caleb didn't know, but he suspected half of it was her unswerving loyalty to Lenora, the company and, under that same umbrella, himself.

Martha spun back toward her desk. "I didn't say you had to splash your private life all over the magazine," she said. "But it would be nice if you got honest with the press. And with yourself. Maybe once you do, you'll find some peace."

Peace. That didn't exist for him. Maybe never would.

"I'm fine." But even as he said the words, he knew they were a lie. And knew Martha was right. He had been floundering at the head of this company for months, searching for the solutions that would turn it around, and he had yet to find them. Martha would tell him it was because he had yet to straighten out the mess of his personal life, so how could he expect to tame the corporate one?

"You want to know what made your mother so successful?" Martha asked as she typed away on her keyboard.

"She knew what she was doing."

Martha laughed. "No. She didn't. I was here with her from day one, and she was as lost as a puppy on a cat farm. She made a million mistakes. But what she did that made her succeed was put her heart into this company. Into every design she created. That showed, and that's what customers responded to. And she wasn't afraid to ask other people for help once in a while."

"Martha, I'm putting everything I have into LL Designs."

"Everything but your heart."

Caleb shook his head, and his gaze went back to his mother's portrait on the far wall. "That's the one thing I can't afford to put into this company."

"Where the hell have you been?" Karl stood over Sarah's desk, arms crossed over his chest, face an angry mask. "And why the hell are you wearing the exclusive, one-of-a-kind, not-supposed-to-be-seen-by-the-public Frederick K shoes?"

"I have a great explanation," Sarah said. Across the cubicle, Pedro raised an eyebrow in disagreement.

"And that is?"

Sarah scrambled for something to tell her boss. Something that wouldn't make him explode. "Remember how you told me I could write a story on the shoes?" she said, rising out of her seat to make her point. "Well, I thought I could work on it at home—" A partial lie. "—so I took them home the other day. And, uh, my sister accidentally threw one out the window."

"Your sister *accidentally* threw a Frederick K stiletto out the window?" Karl's brows peaked in twin triangles. "Did she mistake it for bird food?"

"It all worked out, though, because someone found the shoe."

"Don't tell me. Cinderella? One of the seven dwarves?"

"Caleb Lewis."

The name hung in the air for a long time. Karl's scowl dropped off his face, and then a predatory smile darted across his lean, sharp features. "Oh, really? Well, isn't that interesting?"

She could see Karl formulating the headlines in his mind already. Undoubtedly, every mental word was geared toward shedding the worst possible light on Caleb Lewis—the one that also sold the most issues. "And as soon as I found out, I retrieved the shoe." She left off everything that had happened in between. And certainly didn't talk about the kiss they had shared this afternoon.

That insane, heady, amazing kiss.

One she'd been unable to forget—and unable

to come to terms with. What had she been thinking?

She hadn't been. She'd let the shoes overpower her common sense. That was all. Nothing more.

Uh-huh. Then why was she still thinking about kissing Caleb Lewis? And wishing that kiss had never ended?

Karl pointed at her feet. "None of that explains why you are wearing them now."

She'd forgotten her regular shoes back in Caleb's office but telling Karl that meant explaining everything that had happened between her and Caleb. She'd run out of there so fast, she hadn't realized that she was still wearing the designer stilettos. "I, uh, wanted to write an article on how the shoes make a woman feel. How they can transform her personality."

Karl opened his mouth as if he was going to scream at her. Then he thought a second, and nodded twice. "I like that idea. It's different."

"Good." Sarah hoped her voice didn't betray her relief that Karl had agreed with her.

"And you…you're a good candidate for that kind of transformation thing."

"Because I'm not a supermodel?"

"Because you're a regular woman." He gave her shoulder a pat. "The kind a guy could have a beer with."

Wow. Rousing endorsement for her femininity. If anything could make her feel less like a supermodel, that was it. Except, with the shoes on her feet, Sarah realized Karl's words didn't pack any ego punch. "Gee, thanks, Karl."

"Run with that idea, then come talk to me. Might make a good feature," Karl said, and started to leave.

He hadn't promised her the article. She hadn't moved any further away from the gossip pages nor any closer to the main section of the magazine. She could see her best opportunity for the career she wanted stepping away the farther away Karl got. If he wasn't going to let her run with the shoes idea, then she'd just have to hit him with another one until he said yes. "I also wanted to do a piece on Caleb Lewis and LL Designs. In fact, I've been working on it all week while you've been out. He's really doing some amazing things over there."

"That man is practically a one-person gossip machine." Karl turned back, chuckling. "What's our favorite playboy up to now?"

Kissing the reporter who ruined his reputation? Turning my world inside-out and my thoughts into a revolving door of his mouth on mine?

"I meant a *serious* piece. One that would go into *Smart Fashion,* not the tabloid," Sarah said.

"Caleb is taking the company in new directions and really revitalizing it. Readers love that kind of climb-back-to-success story."

Karl chewed on his lower lip. "Maybe. What I'd like is the scoop on Lenora. Where is she while her company is in trouble? Living it up in the South of France? That's the story we should be doing. Just credit some vague 'source,' or 'close friend' saying she's partying like a rock star while her son runs the company into the ground."

Sarah forced herself not to roll her eyes at her boss's insensitivity. "The real story is what Caleb's doing with the company this year, Karl," she said. "He's got some fabulous ideas for a new shoe line and—"

"Fine. I'll get Laura on it."

Laura. The magazine's main features writer, who covered virtually everything in the fashion industry. And whose job Sarah had wanted for years. "Karl, I want to write it."

"You?" His gaze roamed over her. Assessing. Calculating. He rubbed his jaw. "All right. I'll let you have this *one*. But you screw it up—"

"No. I want more. I want both stories." A new kind of strength rose inside her. Not just because of the shoes, but because in the last few days, she'd found a new confidence in herself. In the job she knew she could do with these articles. "I want to do the one on the shoes, too. And after I prove myself to you with these—and I will—I want to be transferred to the main magazine."

"Moxie. I like that." Karl nodded. "You got it, Sarah. But you better do a damned good job, because our fall issue is our biggest seller. The last thing I need is crap on the pages."

"You can count on me."

As Karl walked away, Pedro sent Sarah a thumbs-up and a whispered, "You go, girl." The thrill of victory peaked inside her. She'd done it. Now all she had to do was live up to everyone's expectations—

And hope that kissing Caleb Lewis hadn't made him change his mind about working with her.

CHAPTER SEVEN

CALEB dropped a blank notepad on Sarah's desk, following the wide white pad with a trio of colored pencils. "I want your input."

She glanced up, surprised to see him. Especially after how they had left things in his office the day before. She'd spent that night tossing and turning, replaying the kiss again and again. The way his lips had claimed hers, sent a charge of desire roaring through her body. She was fooling herself if she thought a pair of stilettos was the sole reason she had kissed Caleb Lewis.

She had wanted him for as long as she could remember. However, wanting—and the wisdom of having—were two very different things.

Now he was in her cubicle, sending her tossing and turning in a whole other way.

"My input? On what?" she asked, deciding it was better to steer the course away from the very personal incidents of the other afternoon.

"I want to know what you think." He dropped into the visitor's chair beside her. His tie was loosened, the top button of his shirt undone. He looked relaxed and sexy, as if he could put his feet up beside her at the end of a long day, share a glass of wine and a long conversation.

"Oh. Okay." She tried not to let disappointment trickle into her voice. The last thing she wanted Caleb Lewis to know was that she had been affected by that kiss. Or that she was upset that he had come all the way over to her office—

For work. Not to see her.

He leaned forward, propping an elbow on the arm of the chair. "If you had to describe LL Designs—the company my mother headed, not the one it is now—in three words, what would you say?"

Sarah gnawed on the end of her pen while she thought for a moment. "Adventurous. Spirited. Jeweled."

"Jeweled? You mean with too many rhinestones?"

She laughed. "No. I meant that when a woman put on an LL Designs dress, she felt like a diamond. Or a ruby. Or an emerald. Unique and beautiful."

He shook his head and let out a gust. "That's brilliant. If I had had to describe my mother's designs, I would have said the same thing. Here I am, a former director of marketing, not thinking with my marketing brain. I've been too busy trying to stem the bleeding to think ahead."

"Well, you've faced a lot of challenges in the past year. But you're doing the shoe collection, right? That should be different, something exciting."

He shook his head, not ready to agree. "What did you call our designs? *Lacking in originality, unfocused?* You were right. Absolutely right. And if I don't start thinking in a new direction, everything for the spring collection and the shoe launch will have the same problem. And where will that get me? Nowhere but backwards." He flipped out his cell phone and punched in a few numbers. "Martha, halt production on the spring collection and set up a meeting with the design staff at one. Tell them I want them to think of ideas that are…" His gaze met Sarah's. "Adventurous. Spirited. Jeweled." Then he hung up.

Sarah's jaw dropped. "You're seriously scrapping the entire spring collection based on something I said?"

"It's the smart thing to do. If I release what I have on tap right now, I'll end up exactly where I was before. And that's not progress."

Sarah sat back and smiled at him. This was

not the Caleb Lewis she had expected. In fact, over the last week, he had surprised her over and over again. He was proving himself to be open to input, to change, to risk. "Well, if I didn't know better, I'd say Lenora was back. That's exactly the kind of thing your mother was famous for doing."

"And exactly the kind of thing that threw the company into a panic more than once. It's also something I should have done a long time ago."

"Why didn't you?"

"I've been blind. To what this company needs, to what I should be doing." His gaze drifted to some far-off spot, and she wondered what was going through his mind. "To the choices I need to make."

She heard something in his voice that told her those choices had little to do with the company. "What do you mean?"

He opened his mouth as if he was going to say more, then shut it again. Caleb drew himself up, and seemed to shrug off the heavy cloud hanging over him. "Nothing."

The reporter in her raised its suspicious head. He was hiding something. She'd thought they had come far enough along in their relationship—this was a relationship, right? After those kisses?—that he wouldn't feel compelled to hold back if she asked him a question. Plus, he'd been honest about the company, about his childhood, about the struggles with this year's collection. He'd told her dozens of things.

Why not whatever this was?

Her journalistic instincts nudged at her. Told her to search for the truth, to find the answers that Caleb wasn't giving her.

Before she could ask him anything more, he spoke. "If I'm starting from scratch this close to Fashion Week, I'm going to need some help."

Sarah was busy writing a few notes about this change in direction with LL Designs, and didn't look up at him. "I'd say so. You're going to be busy."

"I meant…I'm going to need you, Sarah Griffin."

"Me?"

Caleb nodded. "You're our target audience. And you have the best analysis of LL Designs that I've heard in a long time."

"But—"

Caleb leaned over, and his hand covered hers. Her words sputtered to a stop. "I need you. Please help."

I need you.

Those three words worked like a magic spell. They were the words Sarah Griffin had never been able to resist. Coupled with Caleb's deep blue eyes, they made saying no not even a possibility. Still, she made an attempt. "I'm supposed to be writing the story."

A smile curved across his face, and everything inside Sarah quivered with desire. To kiss him again. To have him take her in his arms again, and crush her to him. "This time, you're part of the story." Caleb tapped at the blank pad of paper he'd dropped on her desk. "I know you love shoes. And I know you know a lot about them—just from working here, and from the snippets of conversation I've heard between you and the shop owners in the last few days. You've impressed me, Sarah."

"That's the last thing I ever expected to hear you say about me."

"Ditto." He grinned. "You are a good reporter. You ask incisive questions, you listen, you observe, and you put all of that together and make informed judgments. I have no doubt that the story you're doing on the company will be the best one ever written."

The warmth of his praise filled her. All these years, she had worked at the tabloid, sure she could be something better, wanting to be something more, but never having the opportunity to prove her skills. And here, the one man she had vilified on the pages of *Behind the Scenes* was telling her he thought she wasn't just good, but great. She wanted to hug him.

Instead she picked up the pad of paper. "Then what is this about?" She fingered the blank pages.

"I think you're smart on more than one kind of paper. I'd like to see if you could...design."

"Design?" She shook her head and moved back in her seat. "Caleb, I don't have any experience in that area. I'm a writer, not an artist."

"You're a creative person. Sometimes that's enough." He pushed the notepaper closer to her. "I've seen your shoe collection. I know you have a passion for this. Just draw what your ideal pair would be."

Pedro popped his head over the cubicle wall, eavesdropping without shame. "Did someone say shoes?"

"Let's go somewhere else to talk about this," she said, gathering the paper and pencils and getting to her feet. The last thing she needed was Karl walking in and finding her collaborating with Caleb Lewis. Or Pedro asking questions that Sarah didn't have answers for.

They ended up at a coffee shop a block down the street, huddled in a corner booth. Sarah had expected Caleb to sit across from her, but he slid in beside her, his hip against hers, his thigh running down her jean-clad one. Heat ignited along the connection, rushing through her veins. The waitress dropped off coffee but Sarah barely noticed. Her every breath centered around Caleb's nearness. Her mind replayed that kiss like a stuck videotape. She watched his mouth move and fantasized about tasting him again, and again.

Oh, this was not good.

"Where do I start?" she asked, dropping her gaze to the blank pages. "I've never done this before. I don't know what makes you think I can create anything."

Caleb picked up a second pencil. His hand skated near hers. "Just draw. Doesn't have to be anything fancy. An idea, really, is all I'm looking for."

She did as he said, and her first attempts were awful. Stilted, rough approximations of footwear that no one would wear. "This is so not my forte."

Caleb's hand covered hers, and Sarah's breath caught. "Let yourself go," he said quietly. "Think with your heart, not your mind."

With him right there, his touch still lingering on her skin, she could barely think at all. But she closed her eyes, and let her brain disconnect from her gut, then opened her eyes again and began to sketch. The drawing wasn't good— she was no Picasso, after all—but the shoe that emerged from beneath the lines of the black pencil wasn't bad.

Caleb smiled. "I like that. I like the bow at the top of strap. And how you echoed that detail on the heel. What kind of fabric do you see this in?"

"Satin?" She paused, then the hesitation left her as she pictured the design on her feet, the finishing touch to a slightly belled dress in a deep jewel tone. "Definitely satin."

"I agree. This is a brilliant start." He slid out of the booth, taking her drawing with him, but leaving the rest of the paper and pencils. "I have to get back to work, but I'd like to take this with me."

"You're not serious. That was just an idea—"

"A good one. I want to see what the guys think."

"Caleb, I really don't think it's a good idea for me to be involved in your business. It's a conflict of interest." She paused. "I think."

"I think—" He leaned in closer and half of her wanted him to kiss her again. "—that this is the perfect opportunity for you to add that little extra something to your story. Not only did you see the production process from start to finish but you were part of it yourself. That creates an unforgettable story."

"Is that all you wanted?" she asked. "The story? The design?"

His gaze connected with hers, and a long moment passed with only the clanking sound of dishes in the kitchen and the low murmur of the few customers at the shop's counter. "I think it's best if that's where we leave it, don't you?"

"Of course," she said. And told herself she wasn't disappointed. At all.

CHAPTER EIGHT

THE taxi stopped in front of the bustling night-club. Lines of people snaked around the outside of the building, everyone jockeying for position with the bouncer. It was a typical Friday night—loud, well-lit and crowded.

Inside, Caleb knew, he'd find the antidote he needed. There'd be enough noise, enough activity, to keep him from dwelling too deep in his head. He could go inside there and spend a few hours perfecting that distance he'd gotten so good at over the past year. He could forget about the problems he was leaving at work, the ones he was leaving in New Jersey and the answers he was avoiding with Sarah Griffin.

Like why he had kissed her. Why he still wanted to kiss her every time he thought about her. And why he kept retreating to the safety of work instead of opening his heart, even a little.

A couple exited the nightclub, and a blast of

loud pop music hit the night air. For the first time, the thought of heading through those doors filled Caleb with distaste. For so many nights—too many—he'd been going into clubs like this one. And for what? Had it brought him any closer to where he wanted to be? Or got him any further away from his bad decisions?

Had all those hours he'd spent surrounded by shallow personalities done a thing for absolving his guilt? Made any of this one bit easier?

Hell, nothing did.

After delivering Sarah's sketch to the other designers and having a quick meeting about the shoe line, he'd left work early to make the long drive to New Jersey, hoping, praying, that once he got there someone would say something other than what they had been saying over and over for the last year. "No change. I'm sorry, Mr. Lewis," as if Lenora's silent, persistent vegetative coma were their fault.

The same two words had been uttered today, almost as soon as he walked through the door. Nevertheless, Caleb spent two hours by his mother's bedside, trying to coax a response of any kind out of her.

No change. There never was.

"You getting out, sir?"

Caleb caught the cabbie's inquisitive gaze in the rearview mirror. "No. I changed my mind."

He rattled off his address, and the cab pulled away from the curb. He wasn't going to find what he wanted in that club. Why keep kidding himself?

Fifteen minutes later, he was back at his apartment, with an overjoyed Mac. Caleb clicked the leash onto the Labrador's collar, and stepped out into the cool night. For an hour, they walked, putting miles on his thoughts. He walked block after block, Mac trotting beside him as they made their way through the still-busy streets of Manhattan. The city never slept and, most nights, neither did he.

He stopped when he realized the neighborhood he had ended up at looked familiar.

Sarah Griffin's building. Several lights burned in the third-floor apartment. She was home. He thought about ringing her doorbell, but really, what excuse did he have for being here? For calling her downstairs?

It was far too late at night to claim he was here for another dinner. For all he knew, she was already getting ready for bed and probably didn't want to see him at all, not after the way he had handled that kiss the other day. He'd thought by turning the discussion to business, he could put some distance between them, maybe limit the impact of that kiss, but he was fooling himself if he thought he had.

That kiss had been imprinted on his memory. Sweet, hot, amazing.

It had been all he could think about when he'd sat next to her in the coffee shop. Every time their legs touched or their hands brushed, he wanted to grab her, kiss her again and not stop until this constant ache was assuaged.

Was that how she felt, too? Had she been as transformed by that kiss as he had? After all these days together, did she see the two of them together in a new light? Or did she see him still as the man on the gossip pages? The heartless playboy only out for a good time?

He could go up there, ring her doorbell and ask. Would she open her door to him? Or shut it again?

He didn't want to find out that the answer was no, not tonight.

Caleb turned to go, then heard the creak of a door opening behind him. Mac let out a bark, and tugged on the leash.

"Caleb?"

He pivoted back. Sarah stood on her stoop, a small white trash bag in her hand. The light above washed over her, brushing her hair with golden highlights, and emphasizing the wide dark pools of her emerald eyes. Even in dark blue sweats and a V-necked white T-shirt, she looked beautiful. Sexy. "We were, uh, in the neighborhood," he said, raising the leash in explanation. "I was going to ring the bell, but it was pretty late."

"Did you need to talk to me about something? If it's about that drawing for the shoe, I told you I'm really not an expert at that."

"The sketch was great. And I'm not here about that."

She came down the stairs and stuffed the trash bag into a plastic rubbish container, then shut the lid. "Then why are you here?"

I don't know didn't seem like a valid reason. *I was wandering the city and ended up here* didn't, either. But really, what excuse did he have?

"I…I wanted to see you." If she asked him why, he'd have to delve into a lot of reasons that went deeper than just desire. There was something about Sarah Griffin—something frank and honest—that called to him and had drawn his steps here, instead of anywhere else in the city. That made him want to be honest with himself and finally confront all those issues that he'd done nothing but avoid.

But she didn't ask why. Instead, she just smiled. "Do you want to come up for a while? My dad is down at O'Reilly's with a few of his old buddies from the force. And I'm…" Her voice trailed off.

"Alone?" One word sent his thoughts down paths they had no business visiting. But travel they did, along with his gaze past her eyes, over her lips, down her delicate frame. "If you're sure you want the company..."

He should go. Leave her be. Sarah Griffin was the kind of woman who came with expectations.

She wasn't a model, just out for a good time or a date that could lead her further up the career ladder. No, Sarah was a confident, strong woman who, he was sure, took her relationships as seriously as she did her job.

"I'd love some company," Sarah said, and when she smiled, all those good reasons flew out of his head.

"Great. And if you don't mind a canine companion, too—" He held up the leash again. "—this is Mac."

"Hi, Mac." Her smile broadened. "I love dogs. Come on in, guys." She led the way into the building and up the stairs to her apartment. Mac, already deciding Sarah was a friend, bounded ahead, taking the stairs faster than the humans. He skidded to a stop outside the third-floor apartment door.

Sarah let them all in, then headed for the kitchen. "Do you want a glass of wine? Maybe some crackers?"

"Wine would be great. Thanks."

She poked her head out of the galley kitchen. "I wasn't talking to you." She tossed him a grin. "I was talking to Mac."

Caleb chuckled. "Mac's got a drinking problem, but he doesn't want to admit it, so maybe we should stick to water for him."

Sarah's laughter joined his, and in that moment, Caleb thought how nice it was to share something so simple as a joke with another person. Clearly, he'd spent too much time with people who had little in common with him. He unclipped Mac's leash, then laid it on the hall table. The dog trotted over to the space in front of the heating vent and lay down, settling his head on his paws.

Caleb followed Sarah, and took a stance against the counters, watching her move around her kitchen, efficient and fast. She pulled a chilled bottle of white wine out of the fridge, followed by a block of Colby cheese, then sliced the cheese and added it to a platter flanked by large, buttery crackers. A stem of red globe grapes joined the cheese.

"Let me make myself useful," Caleb said. He reached for the wine, then screwed in the opener and popped the cork.

"Thank you." Sarah placed two wineglasses beside him. The jasmine notes of her perfume mingled with the fruity tones in the wine. He was tempted, so tempted, to lean over and kiss the hollow of her throat, then trail his mouth down the V of skin exposed by her shirt. To draw her into his arms, and press her body to his, to feel those curves under his hands. Again. And this time, not let go.

The wine splashed a bit as Sarah poured, her hand unsteady, and he wondered if she was just as affected by their close proximity as he was. Either way, she didn't stay to find out—she picked up the glasses, and headed out of the room, Caleb following behind. They took up seats on the loveseat and sofa, the platter and glasses sitting on the glass coffee table between them like a barrier. Mac got to his feet and lumbered over to them, positioning himself under the coffee table—ready to retrieve any crumbs.

"I bet you're wondering why I'm not at the opening of that new club on the east side," Caleb said.

"Well..." Sarah picked up her wineglass, but didn't sip. "Yes."

"Were you going to cover it for the magazine?"

She shook her head. "No. Someone else is handling my column while I work on the story about LL Designs."

"So you're done reporting on my shenanigans?"

"For now."

The happiness he'd felt a second ago dissipated. But what did he expect? That she would just quit her job at the tabloid because they'd shared a couple of meals? A kiss?

Still, he wondered why she worked there at all. She was so clearly another kind of woman, not at all the type he expected to be wasting her days at a tabloid.

Sarah put the glass back on the table. "So, why aren't you there tonight?"

"I went over there," Caleb said, "but never got out of the cab."

Her brows arched in surprise. "Really? Why?"

"I've had enough of that life." Martha was right. It was time he got honest with himself, and if that honesty made it into print, so be it. He met Sarah's eyes, and saw in them genuine interest, not a woman taking mental notes to use in the next day's column, and a feeling of trust filled him. "Every time I went to one of those clubs, I thought I'd find…something."

Confusion knitted her brows. "A woman?"

He let out a gust. "No. I'm the last person who should be trying to have a relationship."

She sat back, as if putting distance between him and the sentence. "Oh."

"I should be concentrating on the company instead." Then why was he staring at her lips, and thinking constantly about having Sarah Griffin in his arms again? Why couldn't he put her from his mind?

"True," she said. "But even a CEO deserves a social life. And from what I've seen and learned in the last week, you work an incredible amount of hours. More than I thought."

"I'm not all parties and martinis, is that it?"

"Not at all."

"Maybe you're right." But not in his eyes. If he had his priorities straight, he would be putting in every hour he could at that cherry desk. Working until the profit margins increased and every general ledger showed LL Designs in the black. If he was the kind of CEO his mother would want and expect him to be, he would have put the company first and his life second.

As she had.

But what had that cost her? No man in her life. No time for friends or family. She'd spent more hours behind that desk than she had with her only child. And when she wasn't at work, she was talking about work, even sketching ideas on restaurant napkins and taking pictures of images she thought would make great fabrics later. His mother's life had been entirely skewed toward work.

Was balance achievable? Or did he have to do what she had done in order to keep the company afloat?

Thinking of his mother sent a pang of guilt through his chest. He got to his feet and crossed to the window, watching the traffic go by as he sipped his wine. Even through the closed windows, he could hear the soft flup-flup-flup of tires running over the pavement, the low purr of the cars' engines. From somewhere down the street, someone laughed, the high-pitched sound carrying on the evening breeze.

Silence extended between them. Sarah was undoubtedly watching him. What was she seeing? The wild playboy from the gossip pages? The incompetent CEO whose company was slipping out of his grasp? Or a man struggling to do the right thing, even after he'd forgotten what that right thing was?

"Can I ask you something?" she said.

He nodded.

"And this is for me, not the magazine. I don't want you to think anything you say to me when we're not doing an official interview will end up making it onto the cover."

He didn't turn away from the window. Not yet. "I trust you, Sarah."

"That means a lot," she said, and her voice broke a little.

Now he did turn toward her, and close the gap between them. "What?"

"I've just been working there so long that it feels like I sold my soul. And you just reminded me that I'm still in here, and that the Sarah Griffin I wanted to be is still possible."

"Why have you spent so many years working a job that you hate?"

She held the wineglass, and stared at the pale-yellow liquid for a long time. "I had to. Someone had to pay the bills. Someone had to be responsible. It was the only job that let me work nights, go to college during the day and have flexible enough hours to check on my dad and my sister. One year turned into two, into three, and before I knew it, I was entrenched there. It was easier to stay than move on."

"And now?"

"Now I'm thinking about new paths. But it's..." She sighed. "...scary."

He lowered himself onto the sofa beside her. "I know all about scary. I've been terrified since the day I sat in my mother's chair and took over the company. I've been so sure I would ruin the whole thing. Now, with this shoe line and throwing out the spring designs, I'm going down new paths, and it could all backfire as easily as it could succeed."

"I think it'll all work out."

He grinned. "I'm glad someone's feeling confident." He took a sip of wine, then sat back against the sofa. "My mother always had this air about her that everything would work out. Even if she was secretly afraid it wouldn't. I think it was because she'd never done anything else but this business."

"She started when she was a teen, right?"

He nodded. "She used to wear all her own creations to school, and before she knew it, her friends were asking her to make some things for them. It was after she had a waiting list for prom dresses that she realized she could make a career of this. She went to school, got her degree in fashion, all the while keeping up this little business on the side. And after she graduated, she started LL Designs."

"And your father? Was he involved?"

"My father was a news reporter." Caleb paused, then spat out the other part of his personal history, his mother's warnings sounding again in his head. *Don't trust the media—ever.* But Sarah was different, he was sure of it. "He was also a married man."

"Oh."

"Yeah. My mother found that out the same

day she found out she was pregnant with me. He wanted nothing to do with her or the baby, so from day one, it was just her and me."

"That must have been so hurtful. I can't even imagine."

"My mother may have been a single parent, but she was a fabulous one."

"Is she enjoying retirement?"

He paused. Here was his opening, his opportunity to tell her the truth. Surely, she, of all people, would understand.

But would she? How many people really understood the agonizing decision of whether to let a loved one go? The weeks and months of watching his mother linger in a non-existence? Would Sarah see the painful reality of his choices, or would she recoil from him, and tell him he wasn't the son she'd thought he was all along?

"I think my mother's happy," he said, the words scraping past his throat.

"And what about you?"

"Me?" He let out a breath. "I don't have time to think about that."

"Then why not just sell to Frederick K and get out of this business altogether?"

If there'd been a list of top ten questions Caleb thought Sarah would ask him, that one wouldn't even have made it to the list. But he realized it made sense. He was struggling at the helm of

LL Designs, and he had a ready buyer. Selling was the easiest path of all. "Because I won't sell my mother's hard work to that idiot."

For one, his mother would be horrified to know her son had given up her life's work to someone else. For another, Caleb had no doubts that Frederick K wanted to buy the company simply to see it disappear off the face of the earth. And most of all, Caleb had taken on a challenge when he'd accepted the role of CEO. Selling out to Frederick K would mean he had failed.

And he wasn't going to do that. LL Designs would continue to be owned by a Lewis if it killed him.

"And yet..." Sarah clasped her hands and rested them on her knees, and he could tell she was gearing up to say something he didn't want to hear. "...although you work hard, and I know you care a lot, there are times that you aren't as invested in the company as maybe you should be."

He snorted. "Are you kidding me? I spend every waking hour there."

She arched a brow.

"Okay, maybe not the night ones."

"How much of a leader do you think you are when you come in the next morning, after spending hours and hours at a nightclub?" She put up a hand to stop his objections before he could voice them. "I'm not trying to be mean, but it's like you're this contradiction, and even you don't seem to know which side of the sentence you want to be on. I've seen what you can do. I've heard the praises from the customers you deal with, the workers on the factory floor, the other people in management. They all think you're great. But there's little piece of you missing. And I think it's because you're holding a little bit back. You can't be an effective company leader if you're also trying to be bachelor of the month."

He scowled. "I told you, I'm done with that life."

A soft smile curved across her face. "I heard you say the same thing two months ago."

"I did?" He thought back, and couldn't remember a single conversation he'd had with Sarah or any of the other reporters. "Not to you."

"To one of your friends as you were walking out of that club in the East Village."

He thought of the place on 21st Street that he liked to frequent. Every once in a while, one of his college buddies or one of the guys he used to work with at the marketing agency would tag along. The club was famous for its wooden dance floor, decadent martinis, energetic patrons. The night Sarah was talking about had been late in the summer. He'd gone out with one of his college friends, a guy named Rick, but Caleb had left early—for him, at least. He'd ducked out of there somewhere around eleven, just as the crowds were starting to fill the place. Rick had tried to argue him into staying longer, but Caleb had been adamant.

"I did say that," he said as the memory came back. "I hadn't realized you were there."

A slight smile crossed her face. "That's where I always seem to be, in the shadows."

He leaned forward, his gaze meeting hers. "Why?"

"Why was I there? Because the magazine pays me to be. I—"

"I meant why are you always in the shadows?"

"This isn't about me. I was asking about you and why you said that two months ago."

"Answer my question and I'll answer yours."

"That's not playing fair."

"I'm the bad boy, remember? I'm not supposed to play fair."

She laughed, but the sound was short-lived. Sarah got to her feet, and crossed to a CD player on the shelf. She toyed with the selection of music, as if looking at the albums of Norah Jones and Colbie Calliat would provide the words she sought. "It's easier," she said finally, the words so soft he almost didn't hear them.

"Easier than what?"

She opened one of the Norah Jones CDs and inserted the shiny disc into the player, then turned it on. Soft bluesy tones filled the apartment. "Easier than being a part of that world."

He rose, and came up behind her. His hands ached to reach out and touch the silky strands of her chocolate-colored hair, but he held back. Didn't touch her. "Why?"

She turned to him, and that smile appeared on her face again, weaker this time. "Isn't that like ten questions to my one?"

"You keep answering with very short sentences. Ones that don't tell me anything."

Like why she had hung around the world he had dived into with the enthusiasm of a lifetime swimmer. Like why she had never joined in on any of the parties at the clubs, even though he'd seen her get invited over and over again by the dozens of people in the industry who knew who she was. Always, she'd used the excuse of working, but Caleb didn't buy it.

"If you'd really been seeking that exclusive scoop that would pull you out of the gossip pages, you would have accepted those offers to sit at the tables with the powers that be," he said. "But I never saw you do it. Why?"

"You watched me?" Surprise lit her eyes. "Noticed me?"

He reached up and captured her jaw, unable to keep his hands away from her for one more second. God, she was beautiful. Enchanting. "Every time."

"Just so you knew where your nemesis was?"

He laughed. "Partly. But partly because you intrigued me."

"Me?" She let out a gust. "Yeah, right."

"You did. I wondered whether you were some kind of nun or someone very committed to her job. Or…"

"Or what?"

"Or involved with someone."

Now it was her turn to laugh. "Oh, yeah. In all my spare time, I'm going to have a relationship, too?"

His thumb traced over her lower lip and she opened her mouth against his touch. The sarcasm dropped from her features, and her eyes widened, locked on his. Why hadn't some smart man snapped her up already? Why was she as alone as he was? "Why not?"

Sarah swallowed hard, and in the background, Norah Jones sang a melody about temptation and love. "Because my family needs me and I have the job and…"

"Excuses." He should know; he'd been using the same ones for years to justify his one-night interactions with the models that flocked around him. A few drinks, a spin on a dance floor, and more often than not, he went home alone, unentangled.

"And who would I have a relationship with?"

Her question hung between them, asking something neither of them wanted to come out and say. But both of them had clearly thought. Get involved with each other? Or not?

"I know this CEO of a fashion house…" Caleb said, unable to take his gaze off hers or to release her. Everything inside him pounded with the same insistent message—

Kiss her. Kiss her.

"You do?"

He nodded. Slow. "And he might not come with the best personal recommendations when it comes to relationships, if you believe the tabloids, but I hear he's not so bad in person."

She shook her head. Slow. Her silky skin slid against his fingers, so, so tempting. "No, he's not so bad, not at all."

"Then maybe you should give him a try."

Now a new smile curved on her lips, one that

teased and tempted him. "I believe I already did that."

"Ah, yes. I remember that. Very well." He brought his face closer to hers, until his mouth was only a millimeter away from hers, until they were sharing the same breath. "Perhaps you should do that again. Just to make one-hundred-percent sure, of course."

"Perhaps," Sarah breathed, and before one more second of agonizing want passed—

Caleb kissed her.

Desire surged through him the second their lips met, and instead of the tender embrace he'd planned, Caleb found his arms going around Sarah's body. She fumbled to put the wineglass on the shelf, the crystal goblet nearly toppling and sloshing both of them with drops of chardonnay. Then her fingers wove through his hair, pulling him closer, closer still, until Caleb couldn't tell where he began or she ended.

Their kiss was fire, tongues dancing and intertwining, lips claiming one another. He crushed her to him, feeling the smooth temptation of her breasts between the soft fabric of their T-shirts. He pulled back just enough to slide a hand between them and under her shirt, drifting over the creamy expanse of her belly before his hand claimed one breast, fingers cupping the soft round flesh, his thumb tracing over the sensitive nipple. She arched against him and let out a gasp. Her pelvis pressed against his erection, and in that moment, Caleb thought for sure he'd go insane if he stopped touching Sarah.

"Caleb," she whispered, his name sounding deep and throaty. "Oh, God, Caleb, we shouldn't—"

"Mmm...probably not." He dipped his head to taste the sweet skin of her throat while his hand continued to play with the sensitive peak of her breast. Sarah pressed into him even more.

"No, seriously. We, uh, really need...to...stop."

Something about her tone made him draw back. He connected with her gaze and saw that she was serious. "Why?"

"Because we're working together and I don't want to taint what I write with a personal relationship with you."

He grinned. "Are you saying I'm a conflict of interest?"

"In every way possible." She let out a sigh, then slipped away from him. "Let's be real, Caleb. Even if we didn't have this article as an obstacle..." She paused, then met his gaze. "I'm not your type."

"How do you know what my type is?"

"I've been photographing it and writing about it for a year."

"Those are not the kind of women I want to have a relationship with. You are."

A smile surged across her face. "Really?"

He nodded. "Really, really."

She pressed a quick kiss to his mouth, then drew back, a question in her eyes. "Then we're back to my original question. Why are you out every night if you don't want to be and these aren't the kind of people you want to spend your time with?"

He let out a long breath. He'd just told Sarah he wanted to have a relationship with her, and in a relationship, people were open. Honest. About everything, even their worst faults. And their worst choices.

If he told her the truth, how would she react? Would she ask him to leave? Or would she understand that he was merely a man who was wrestling with an impossible decision? "Like you said, it's easier."

"Than dealing with the problems at the company?"

"Something like that." If he stayed any longer, he'd do one of two things—kiss her again, and she'd made it clear that she didn't want him to do that unless he answered her question—or tell her the real reason he went clubbing all the time.

So he didn't have to make the agonizing decision to let his mother go.

He crossed the room, picked up the leash. At the sound, Mac scrambled to his feet and hurried to his master's side, dropping into a sit to wait for the leash to be attached. "I should go. It's late and if I stay..."

"We'll probably end up right where we were before."

He nodded. "And you're right. We shouldn't do this." He couldn't, not without being honest with her, which was only fair. And right now, he'd rather leave than see the look in her eyes when he gave her the answer she wanted.

Caleb clicked the leash onto Mac's collar, then headed out of Sarah's apartment and back into the cold, lonely night.

CHAPTER NINE

THE factory was humming with a new energy, one Caleb hadn't seen in years. As he walked the floor, he heard the buzz from the employees—they were overwhelmed by the additional work, but excited about the new designs, ones that he and his team had put together with inspiration from Sarah's shoe design. He'd tacked it up in the conference room and told them to build the collection around the satin high heel. At first, the team had thought he was crazy, then they'd gotten to work and had dozens of new ideas by the end of the day. That buzz extended to Caleb, too, and his steps held a new energy. He had a good feeling about this collection. A damned good feeling.

And it was all thanks to Sarah Griffin. If he hadn't asked her opinion, he'd be putting out the same tired product as before. But that wasn't what he thought about when he thought of her. No, his mind drifted to her smile, her eyes, the way her face lit up when she laughed. It had been years since he'd spent his days thinking about a woman, her presence lingering in the back of every sentence he spoke, every move he made. He was already wondering how long it would be until he saw her again.

"I think you've done it," Martha said.

"Done what?"

"Brought this company back from the dead." Then Martha's blue gaze softened and she laid a hand on his shoulder. "Sorry, Caleb. Bad joke."

"It's fine." He cleared his throat. "I'm glad to see things are back on track. I really think these new designs will do it for us. They're bold, bright and—"

"Not quite what your mother would have done."

Caleb stopped walking and looked at Martha. "What do you mean, not quite what she would have done? That's exactly what I was going for."

"Lenora was an amazing designer, don't get me wrong, but she had a tendency to run a one-woman shop. She was the vision for this company, the one who created everything herself. She chose every element, right down to the thread they used in the sample pieces. She had designers, yes, but they weren't used for much more than translating her ideas onto paper."

Caleb thought back to the Saturdays he'd spent here as a little boy, playing trucks on the floor of the very office he now occupied. The summers he had spent working here, both while he was in high school and during college. Martha was right—it had been the Lenora show, every year. Every collection.

His mother's creative genius was unmatched, except by her need to control every element of the production process. He'd thought it was because she wanted to ensure quality and perfect execution of her vision, but he realized now that it had been part of her personality. As well as something that hurt the company in the long run because LL Designs lost one too many smart and talented people who were frustrated because they weren't being heard or utilized. "Do you think that's why two of them left just before she got ill?"

Martha nodded. "They wanted a chance to shine on their own. To actually design."

"I can understand that," Caleb said.

"The designs you and the team came up with yesterday are collaborative," Martha said. "They have that feel of…" She paused, searching for the right words. "…being created to appeal to a broad audience."

"You trying to tell me nicely that they're cookie-cutter?"

Martha laughed. "Not at all. Rather a wider variety of offerings. Something for everyone. And, you've managed to incorporate the flair that LL Designs is known for. Not to mention, you weren't afraid to bring in an outsider for an opinion. Brilliant, if you ask me."

Caleb basked in the praise. For a year, he'd been struggling in the top spot. Most days he felt like he had no idea what the hell he was doing. He'd come over to the company from a totally different field with a lot of good intentions and not a lot of fashion experience. Coupled with the constant worry about his mother, the stress of the last year had been a heavy load for Caleb to bear, and there were days when he'd thought he couldn't do it one more second.

But now, it seemed things were finally turning around. As if he had hit his stride. "I have Sarah Griffin to thank for that. She got me thinking in a new direction. Well, not new, but rather, the way I used to think when I was a creative director. If one brain isn't doing the job, bring in outside brains and tap the talent you already have. We'd have meetings once a month in the pit, as we called it. No idea was too off-the-wall or bad. We found that a couple hours of collaborative thinking brought out some of the coolest ideas."

"So how is this 'collaboration' going?" Martha asked, putting air quotes around the word.

"Great. You're seeing it at work right now." He waved toward the busy factory floor. "And over there, they're starting the prototype for the shoe line. It should be—"

"I meant with Sarah Griffin."

That was a question that required a much more complicated answer than the one he'd just given. How were things with him and Sarah?

Well, if those kisses were any indication, things between him and Sarah were hot— and heating more by the day. She was the first woman in a long time—maybe ever—that he found himself looking forward to seeing. Wondered about when she wasn't with him.

Sarah Griffin had gotten under his skin, and he was damned glad. He was thinking about things he hadn't thought about in a long time— like a future.

"That's...developing," Caleb said.

Martha chuckled. "Is that a smile I see on your face? Are we going to have some Lewis babies running around here someday soon?"

Caleb backed up, putting up his hands to ward off Martha's words. "Whoa. Let's not get ahead of ourselves. All I did was kiss her." A foolish grin filled his face, and a lilt of joy simmered in his gut. "Twice."

Martha's hand landed on his shoulder again. "I think you've changed more than just the company, Caleb. And if you ask me, it was about damned time."

The scoop broke over the next day. Headlines everywhere, blaring at Sarah as she walked to work.

Famous Designer on Deathbed. Callous Son Leaves Lenora Lewis to Die. Couture Queen in Coma.

Sarah's steps sputtered to a stop as she took in the headlines from several publications, the words hitting her like punches. Each publication said pretty much the same thing. Sarah knew how it worked—one magazine got the story, the others rushed to blast the same scoop on their pages. It was an incestuous business, with each trying to top the other for better newsstand sales. She skimmed the competition's front pages, thinking in her head about which ones had hit the street first, who had the earliest deadlines, trying to figure out the pack leader for the story. She stopped when she got to *Behind the Scenes*.

Lenora Lewis at Death's Door while Son Parties!

Sarah gasped, yanked the tabloid off the pile, and skimmed the article. According to the "source," one of the employees at the rehab center in New Jersey where Lenora Lewis was being treated, the famous designer had been in a coma for a year, while Caleb Lewis went about his life. "He just ignores her," the staffer said. "I'm sure it pains her."

Lenora was in a coma? Not retired at all? And Caleb hadn't told her? Why?

"You going to buy that, miss?" the tall dark-haired man behind the counter asked, gesturing at the tabloid. "Because this ain't a library, you know."

"Uh, yes." Sarah dug in her pocket for a few bills, then added the other tabloids to the pile before paying. She headed to work, flipping open the article from *Behind the Scenes* to read that first.

She read it twice, three times, sure that it wasn't Lenora's name she was seeing at all. But no, it was. Caleb had kept a huge secret from her. There was only one reason why he would do such a thing.

Because despite everything they had gone through together in the week and a half they had spent with each other, he still didn't trust her. At heart, he still saw her as the gossip reporter.

As she read the pieces, she was more and more sure that *Behind the Scenes* had been the one to break the story, and the others had followed, like vicious dogs nipping at the publication's heels. But the real question was who had written the piece for *Behind the Scenes?* Why? And where had they gotten the information?

She stopped dead on the sidewalk when her gaze fell on the byline.

By Sarah Griffin.

Oh, God. How could this have happened? She hadn't written this article. Not one word. Why would Karl attribute it to her? Sarah stuffed the tabloids into her tote bag and hurried down the sidewalk toward the twelve-story building that housed the *Smart Fashion* publication family. She bypassed her cubicle—

And went straight to Karl's office.

"What the hell is this?" She slapped the article on his desk. "Why is my name on this? I didn't write it."

"It's your column. Who cares if you wrote it?" Karl took a bite out of the blueberry muffin beside him. A purple smear lingered on the corner of his mouth.

"I didn't have anything to do with it. That's lying."

Karl threw up his hands. "I swear, you writers are impossible to keep happy. You weren't here, you were off writing that 'real' piece you wanted to do, so when the information came in, I had one of the interns do it. You'll have to split the pay for the piece, of course, but the byline is the biggest part."

She imagined Caleb's reaction when he saw her name on the piece, and how he would think that she had betrayed him. "Do you know what this is going to do to my life?"

A smile crossed Karl's face, and for a moment, Sarah was reminded of the Cheshire cat. "It's going to make you the most famous gossip reporter in this town. Isn't that everybody's dream, baby?"

Caleb was twenty feet from the office when the pack of reporters descended on him, shouting questions about his mother, angling in closer, hoping for a remark. What the hell? How did they find out about her condition? He said only two words, "No comment," then headed into the office.

Martha's face shimmered with sympathy. "I put it on your desk."

She didn't have to say what it was. He knew

exactly what she meant, and a big part of him didn't want to see it, read it or deal with it. He'd always known this day would come, that the media would put the pieces together at some point. The headline hit Caleb before he even reached his desk.

Lenora Lewis at Death's Door while Son Parties!

The black-and-white claims glared back at him. From the cover of the one magazine he'd thought he could trust.

Behind the Scenes.

He jerked open the tabloid, so sure he was wrong. She couldn't have. She wouldn't have. Not after everything they'd talked about. Everything they'd shared. Had she just been using all that as a cover? To spy on him? On his mother?

The betrayal ripped through his heart. He'd thought he could trust her.

But there, in print for the entire world to see, were the three words he couldn't believe: By Sarah Griffin. Caleb dropped into his chair, the treachery a sharp blade along his senses. He'd believed she was different. Hell, he'd started to fall for her. Hard.

Had he been blinded by his emotions? Been

distracted by kissing her? Or had she just been one hell of a good liar?

A pang rose in his chest, and he refused to call it hurt. He'd let her into his world, his business, his life, and this was how she repaid him?

She'd done this for one reason only—to advance her own career. He'd been wrong about Sarah Griffin, on every single level.

He picked up the tabloid, headed out of the building again, and straight for the offices of the magazine. This time without any chocolates or good humor. He had one mission and only one in mind—destroy Sarah Griffin.

Sarah typed until her fingers hurt. She pored over her notes from the last few days, scoured the morgue of old articles on LL Designs, and pulled up everything that had ever been written about the company by the competing publications. By eleven, the article was coming together, and Sarah finally felt that she had something that could mitigate the damage done by the tabloid.

She couldn't write fast enough, as far as she was concerned. Undoubtedly, Caleb had already seen the articles and was blaming her. Before she tried to explain, she wanted to show him that she wasn't that writer. That her intentions were true. Surely, he would listen to reason.

But what if he didn't?

"How could you?"

She wheeled around. Caleb Lewis stood beside her desk, his face an angry mask. Damn. He'd seen it and jumped to the only possible conclusion—that she had written it, purposely hurting him. He probably thought she'd been betraying him all along. Oh, how was she going to fix this? "I didn't have anything to do with it, Caleb."

"*No one* knew this information." He leaned in toward her. "*No one*. The only person I let get close enough to me was you. I don't know how you found out or why you went digging into my mother's personal business."

"I swear, Caleb, I had nothing to do with this," she said again. "I didn't even write it."

He snorted. Clearly, he didn't believe her. "Then where did the information come from?"

"I have no idea. My editor said he got a tip and gave it to an intern to write. He put my name on the piece because it's my column. It was wrong, and if I'd known I would have stopped him." Damn. That didn't sound good or even believable.

Caleb shook his head, disgust washing over his features. "Are you trying to tell me this was just one big huge misunderstanding?"

The sarcasm in Caleb's voice stung. How was she ever going to get him to understand? How could she make up for the damage these articles were doing, and would continue to do, now that the pack of media vultures would be pecking away at Caleb for the rest of the story?

"Caleb, I—"

"I don't know why I ever trusted you. Why I ever thought you were different." He threw the tabloid onto her desk. The pages fluttered open, then slid to the floor, a jumbled mess of printed headlines and speculations. "You're like all the rest of them. You use every piece of dirt you can to ruin someone else's life and then call it your job."

She glanced up at him. Yes, what had happened today was a terrible thing, but in her mind, long overdue. She could see the toll this secret had taken on Caleb. How long did he think he could keep this information to himself before some other reporter got hold of it and ran the piece? "Don't you think having the truth out there is better than people speculating? Wondering where Lenora is or how she's doing?"

"My mother wanted privacy. Not this…" He waved at the pages scattered at her feet. "…this mess."

"But now that it's out there, you can deal with

it. People care about Lenora Lewis, and you might find that making the information public will make it easier to cope with her illness. Hiding the truth is never a good idea because someone will always ferret it out."

He snorted. "And what do you know about that? You've spent your life hiding in the corners, writing about other people."

The words stung. She recoiled, her back pressing into the smooth surface of the cubicle wall. "I..."

"Would you want your mother's story splashed across the front page?"

"No, of course not."

"Then what made you think I wanted my mother's in this rag?" He shook his head and let out a gust, not meeting her eyes, not looking at her at all. If anything, that was the worst part. The article had done so much damage that Caleb didn't even want to see her face. "I thought you, of all people, would understand why I wanted to keep this out of the public eye. This decision—"

He cut himself off and swore under his breath.

"What were you about to say?"

"Why? You want to put it in next week's issue?"

"Of course not. I care about you, Caleb." She

reached for him, but he was too far away, and she was sure that if she tried to get any closer, he would leave.

"Yeah? I don't think so. If you did, you'd understand that the decisions I have had to make have been agonizing. Not something I wanted trotted out for all the world to see."

She thought about the article she had read, the things he had mentioned, and a similar decision that had faced her not so long ago. The pieces fell into place. Why Caleb seemed so tortured when it came to his mother. Why he wouldn't want anyone to know about her condition. Why he had stepped in and taken over the company—and refused to give up on it. "Your mother isn't going to get any better, is she?"

He swore again and turned away.

She rose and put a hand on his shoulder. He flinched, but didn't pull away. She took that as a good sign, albeit a small one, but a sign nonetheless. Maybe this wasn't unsalvageable. "Caleb, talk to me. I can help. I've been there."

He spun around and in his eyes, she saw one irrefutable fact, and another truth that Sarah hadn't wanted to accept or believe—everything between them had dissolved in light of that one article. She'd been found guilty of destroying his life—without a trial.

Caleb assessed her for a long silent moment,

his gaze cold, his face hard. "I don't know if I believe that you didn't write that piece of trash. Frankly, I don't care. But I do know one thing. You're not the person I thought you were. I should have trusted my instincts and said the same thing to you that I said to all the other vultures." He leaned in and his blue eyes sparked with anger. "No comment."

The vultures were everywhere. Caleb pulled into the parking lot of the rehab hospital, turned off his car and steeled himself for the pack of reporters waiting outside the hospital. He let out a sigh, put his keys in his pocket and was just about to get out on the driver's side when the passenger's-side door opened and Sarah slipped into his car.

"What the hell are you doing here?"

If she was daunted by his angry outburst, she didn't show it. "I wanted to talk to you."

"Why? So you could get your information before the others?" He gestured toward the pack of reporters milling about the hospital entrance. They toted their cameras and microphones like gladiators preparing for battle. "You want an interview? Or did you just bring along a tape recorder so you can get what you want without me knowing?"

She winced, and he wanted to take the harsh words back. But he didn't.

"I came here to support you," she said.

Had he heard her right? Support him? "Why?"

The car's engine ticked softly as it cooled. Outside, a light rain had begun to fall, washing the windows with a fine mist. The view of the reporters blurred, until he could almost believe they weren't there anymore.

"I know you don't believe I had nothing to do with that article, and that's fine. I'm not here to try and change your mind about that. I'm here because I know what you're going through." Sarah sighed and ran a hand along the center console, as if the words she sought were in the stitched edge of the leather. "In the end, with my mother, we had to make the same torturous decision that you're facing."

"You, your sister and father?"

"My sister was at college by then, and I didn't want to upset her by drawing her into this. My dad…" Sarah shook her head. "He was having a difficult time facing anything to do with my mother. He just tuned out. So ultimately, I was the one who had to make that call. Who stayed until…" She exhaled a shaky breath. "…it was over."

His heart went out to her. In her eyes, he could

read how hard that decision had been for her, how agonizing those last moments must have been. Despite everything, his esteem for Sarah rose several notches. To go through all that, and do it alone? He knew the pain of sitting by a parent's bedside, second-guessing every decision. She'd been younger than him when she'd done it, and she'd still come through okay. Knowing she'd done the right thing.

"I'm sorry," he said. The words seemed useless. Just two words people tossed out there for everything from an inadvertent bump to a major loss. There should be degrees of sympathy words, stronger ones for much bigger traumas. He reached for her, then pulled back at the last moment, not sure where they stood right now, but glad she was there all the same.

Sarah nodded. "Thank you."

His gaze went out the rain-dotted window. The reporters still hadn't noticed his car sitting in the lot. Thank God for that.

He rested his hands on the steering wheel. The hard surface pressed against his palms. Real, solid and something tangible in a day when everything he had to deal with was in his head. He let go, then turned back to Sarah. Was she this woman, the one who was in his car, supportive and caring, or the one who had written that article? Caleb decided he didn't care right now. He needed the supportive Sarah, and he needed her desperately. "So how do you make that decision?"

"There is no litmus test." Her gaze softened. "Sure, the doctors will give you this test result or that one, and medically, it may be a clear-cut answer, but the problem is, your heart doesn't want to hear test results. It wants to hope."

Hope. What a powerful word for just four letters. So tenuous, yet so fragile.

He thought of all the sleepless nights he had spent, weighing the doctors' grave advice against his own undying optimism that maybe they were wrong. "I kept hoping that maybe if I held on long enough…"

"They'd come back with a different diagnosis?"

He nodded, unable to speak. Thick emotion charged through him and his throat closed, choked with tears he had yet to shed. "Damn," he said, and shook his head. "Damn it all."

She reached out and touched him, her hand resting on his arm, a warm, comforting connection. Just…there. For him. He didn't pull away, just absorbed the warmth. "Your mother was a vibrant, powerful woman. Before…this."

A smile crossed his lips. "She was, wasn't she? And after the stroke—" He exhaled. "Everything that was Lenora was gone. She wasn't there anymore. She hasn't been ever since that day."

Sarah's fingers curled around his arm. "Then let her go, Caleb. Don't make her suffer any more."

The hot sting of tears pushed at the back of his eyes, but he didn't let them fall. He couldn't, because it was like giving in, and for so long, Caleb had refused to do that.

"I can't." His gaze met Sarah's. The pain of the last two months rushed to the surface, threatening to tear him apart, forcing him to face everything he had tried so hard to bury with night after night of loud music and mindless chatter. He realized now that he hadn't buried it at all. He had merely let that wound fester in the background until now, it threatened to undo him. "You don't understand, Sarah. I'm the whole reason she's there. She asked me to come by that morning to talk to her about her marketing plan. I thought I could let her wait and show up a little late. My mom was always so buried in her work, she never noticed if I came in ten minutes or two hours late."

Sarah waited for him to continue. Her touch lingered on him, patient, understanding. But no one could understand this...this mistake he had made.

"By the time I got there, at least an hour, maybe more, had passed since she'd had the stroke. I called the ambulance, and they rushed her to the hospital, but…" He sighed. "…it was too late. There was nothing they could do."

"Oh, Caleb. That's not your fault." Sarah's soft, understanding voice filled the car's interior, brushed against his heart. "You don't have to keep paying the price for something that was a twist of fate, nothing more."

"No, I should have been there. I should have…" He bit his lip, hard, but that pain did nothing to assuage the pain inside him. "…done something. Been a better son."

Sarah shifted in her seat, and watched the rain slide down the window. The storm had increased in intensity, and the mist had become fast, fat drops covering everything around them. "When I was a little girl, I used to think if I behaved well enough or I prayed hard enough, God would come along and make my mother better. That maybe this was some kind of cosmic punishment for my mistakes, or that God was waiting for me to prove how much I wanted my mother to be better. It was a long, long time before I finally accepted that her health had nothing to do with me. Or my actions. Hearts give out, Caleb, blood clots explode and cancer multiplies, because…"

"Why?" he asked when she didn't finish.

She swung back around to face him. A glimmer of tears showed in her eyes. "Just because. That's all. It's not fair, and it's not right, but that's the way things work. Just because."

He digested those words. Was it as simple as that? Even if he had been on time, he'd have seen the same end result? Maybe not then, but later?

Just because. That day had been his mother's time, and he couldn't have averted it if he tried. Since then, his actions had only compounded his regrets. They hadn't made his mother better, hadn't eased her pain, or his.

There was nothing he could do to make her better, to turn back the clock. Not then, not now. For the first time in a year, the bricks of guilt began to lighten. "What do I do from here?"

"What's right." Sarah's hand covered his. "That's the only litmus test you need, Caleb."

He exhaled a long sigh. "I know. It's doing what's right that's so tough." It was the decision he had delayed, time and again. The doctors had told him there was no hope, and yet, Caleb hadn't listened. He'd just kept on hoping for the impossible.

"All this time," he said, "I've been doing what was right for me. What made things easier for me to deal with. Instead of doing what was right for her." The light bulb in his head shone so brightly, he didn't know how he had missed the obvious for so long. "Now I see that there's really only one choice to make."

Her fingers curled around his arm. "Do you want me to go with you?"

He considered her for a moment. "Why would you do that for me?"

A smile wavered on her lips. "Because you're not the story, Caleb. You're…so much more."

He wanted to believe her, wanted to trust that she was the Sarah he had come to know, not the one whose byline he had seen this morning. But that would have to wait.

Right now, he had something else to do. Something he should have done a long time ago. He clasped her fingers. "Thank you, but I think this is something I should do on my own."

"Okay." She pressed a kiss to his cheek, lingering for a moment there, then drew back and got out of the car. Sarah Griffin ran toward her car, the heavy rain swallowing her up and taking her out of Caleb's line of sight.

As he'd expected, the reporters attacked him with questions as soon as he reached the door of the hospital. Once again, he said nothing, just brushed past them and inside. The receptionist glared at him for bringing this mayhem onto the staff. He gave her an apology, and her glare softened slightly.

The door to his mother's room was ajar. The lights were dimmed inside the private suite, and only a small Tiffany nightlight burned on the corner table. It was enough to illuminate the bright bedcovers, the dozens of flowers, the portraits of family members lining the window ledge. Nearly everything in the room had been brought here from his mother's Central Park apartment, as Caleb tried to recreate her home bedroom in this foreign place.

As if having all these things from home would be enough to make her want to wake up or restore her to her former self. Like Sarah, he would have done anything to make that happen. And nothing he had done, nothing he had said, no doctors he had paid, had changed the facts. Maybe Sarah was right, and he just needed to face reality. Things like this happened...

Just because.

He dropped into the wingback chair beside his mother's bed, and watched her for a long time. Her eyes were closed, her jaw slack, as if she was sleeping. So peaceful, so quiet. But as the machines beeped a steady rhythm, and his mother's chest went up and down with the help of the respirator, Caleb knew the truth. It was all an illusion, just like the bedcovers and flowers. This wasn't his mother, not anymore, just as this wasn't her cozy bedroom in Manhattan.

Lenora Lewis had left a long time ago. The doctors had been telling him this for a year, but he'd refused to accept it. Refused to accept that a woman who had been such a force in life could be gone.

He laid his head on the bed, and reached out to cover her cool, limp hand with his own. Every time he came here, it seemed she got thinner, paler, frailer. Like there was less and less of her every day.

"I'm sorry, Mom," he whispered to her. "I'm so sorry."

The machines beeped. The respirator raised and lowered, a soft whoosh with each breath it pumped into Lenora Lewis's lungs. Out in the hall, the sounds of life carried on—people talking, walking the halls, sharing laughs.

He clutched his mother's hand, and now, finally, the tears raced to his eyes and a sob chased up his throat. The tears that Caleb Lewis had never shed began to fall, dropping into small round puddles on the white crisp sheets.

"I love you, Mom," he whispered, and now the

tears blurred his vision until he couldn't see anything but her delicate pale fingers. "Goodbye."

The word tore his heart in two. But still, he stayed. Until there wasn't a reason to stay anymore.

CHAPTER TEN

PEDRO leaned over the cubicle wall between his desk and Sarah's, and plucked a chocolate out of the basket on Sarah's desk. "Hey, where'd all the candy go?"

"I've been eating it." Almost nonstop since yesterday. The chocolate didn't solve her problems, but it sure made everything seem more bearable. Like wondering how Caleb was doing. If he still hated her for that article, or if yesterday had made things better. Hell, she wasn't sure she could make that article better, but she was willing to try.

"You ate almost all of it?" Pedro asked. "There was, like, three pounds there."

"And your point is?" She arched a brow in his direction.

Pedro put up his hands, laughing, then he rested his head on his hands on the cubicle wall and studied her. "Something bothering you, peach?"

"No." She looked at the pile of wrappers beside her. "Yes." She toyed with the Frederick K stilettos sitting on her desk, supposed to be serving as inspiration for the article she was going to write on being transformed by the shoes. So far, she'd barely written a word. "I don't know. I can't seem to..." She searched for the right words. "...find the ending to the story."

"Maybe that's because there's another twist yet to come." Pedro grinned, then gestured at the silver-and-blue paper that had arrived on her desk that morning. "Do I see an invitation to the ball, Cinderella?"

"I don't know if I'm going."

"Why not?"

"Well, Caleb will be there—"

"Exactly. And it'll be the perfect opportunity to show him what a hot mama you can be." Pedro picked up the invitation and flipped it over to read the return address on the envelope. "It came from *him*."

"I know." She didn't know why Caleb had sent her an invitation to the pre-Fashion Week party hosted by several of the top couture designers in New York. Did he mean for her to be his date? Was it some cruel way to get back at her because he still thought she'd written that article? Or was she just on some mass-mailing list from LL Designs and she was reading too much into a piece of paper?

What if she went, and in the end, Caleb still didn't believe her? Seeing him again would only compound the inevitable hurt if they couldn't move past that headline.

She sat down at her desk and reopened the article she'd been working on earlier. As her hands hit the keyboard, she wondered for the hundredth time why she kept working for Karl. The man had no ethics—that article in *Behind the Scenes* about Lenora had proved that. If he did it once, what was stopping him from doing it again?

"I think you should go," Pedro said. "Wear something sexy, something shocking."

She looked at the invitation one more time. If she went, the editors of all the other magazines in the industry would be there. If nothing else, it would be a great networking opportunity.

Yeah, that was exactly why she'd go. To network. Not to see Caleb and find out if there was a chance they could move forward again.

Pedro slid down, then popped back up again. "One more thing, Cinderella. Be sure to wear a killer dress because everyone knows when you make a great entrance, the Prince won't be able to keep his eyes, or his hands, off you."

But what if she got there and Caleb was with

another model? Could she stand seeing him, knowing this Cinderella had no chance with the prince her heart desired?

"Griffin!"

Sarah looked up and saw Karl at the end of the aisle. He strode down the block of cubicles and stopped in front of hers. "You need me, Karl?"

"Great job on that story on LL Designs. We're slotting it in the issue."

Satisfaction roared to life inside her. She'd done it. Written something that had made it into the main magazine. Her gossip days were finally over. "Thanks. Now about that job on the staff of—"

"Later, later. Right now, I've got another story for you. And this time, you can write it up and not have all that ridiculous guilt about whether your byline was really yours or not." He rolled his eyes as if that kind of moral commitment was ridiculous.

"Karl, I—"

He slapped a piece of paper on her desk. A phone number and a name had been scribbled on it. "Call this nurse at the rehab center right away."

"Why?"

"The playboy finally did it. Finally pulled the plug on his own mother and that means the death of Lenora Lewis is going to be big news. Huge. I want you on it, and I want you to get a quote from him. I know you've been seeing him, for the article or…" He winked. "…whatever. That should give you an in with the bad boy of fashion. Allow you to get some really juicy quotes."

Revulsion roiled in her stomach. She wasn't this kind of reporter. She never had been. And she wasn't going to be now. She regretted every one of the gossip articles she'd written. If she could yank them out of print, she would. It might be too late for that, but it wasn't too late to do the right thing. "No."

"It's a simple call. Take you all of five min-utes. And then, yeah, you can do those other pieces you wanted to do." Karl grinned. "If you still want to be Lois Lane after you break one of the biggest news stories in our industry."

"Find someone else to do your dirty work." Sarah picked up the paper and pressed it into Karl's hand. "I quit."

Shock dropped Karl's jaw. "You? Quit?"

A sense of satisfaction filled Sarah. For the first time since she'd been assigned to the gossip pages at *Behind the Scenes,* she felt as if she was making the right decision. She had no plan, no back-up job, not so much as a résumé in the mail, but she didn't feel worried. Her conscience filled with the knowledge she'd finally made a choice she could live with. She'd wake up in the morning proud of the path she'd chosen, instead of cringing at the headlines she'd helped craft. "Yep. I'm done here."

"Are you *insane?*"

"Maybe." She turned and grabbed her purse and the invitation from her desk. Her hand hovered over the pair of Frederick K stilettos, sitting there as inspiration for the article. Let them be someone else's inspiration. She'd gotten everything she needed from those shoes.

Then she turned and walked out of the office, leaving behind a stunned boss, an applauding coworker and a career that had never fully suited her.

Caleb stood in his office, watching the city go by a dozen stories below. The early-evening lights twinkled back at him, a sparkle of life that showed the city really didn't sleep. He let out a long sigh, one that seemed to take with it a dozen pounds of stress.

What was Sarah doing right now? Was she thinking of him?

He sure as hell hadn't been able to stop thinking about her. Ever since he'd met her, she'd lingered in his mind. He should let her go—should forget her. After all, hadn't she proved that she was only after the headline?

Except a part of him wondered if she was telling the truth. If that article had been fabricated by someone else. If that was so, then why use her name?

Was Sarah Griffin the woman who had sat in his car in the rain and comforted him? Or was she the one who had taken his most painful secret and blasted it across the front page?

He'd invited her to the party to find out. If she showed up with her reporter pad, then he would know she was the woman who wanted only the headline. If she left that behind, and came as just Sarah...

"You did the right thing."

He turned at the sound of Martha's voice. "Did I?"

"Of course you did. It was a hard decision to make, but the only one you could." The assistant came into his office. "For a year, the doctors have been telling you to let her go."

"But what if..." Those thoughts still plagued him, but not as much as before. It was as if his brain was finally accepting that he had made the right choice. The only one. He glanced over at the portrait of his mother, and he could swear she smiled right at him, as if in agreement with Martha.

You did the right thing.

"There weren't any what-ifs left, Caleb, and you knew that."

He sighed again. "I guess I finally accepted it." Thanks to Sarah's advice and wisdom, and her clearer head. If she hadn't come along yesterday, would he have had the fortitude to make that long walk down the hospital corridor? If he hadn't known she had gone through the same thing, and come out okay?

"Then do one more thing for me," Martha said. "For your mother."

"What's that?"

She pressed a card into his hand. "Live your life. Actually *live* it. Don't watch it from the sidelines. Not anymore."

CHAPTER ELEVEN

"You are obsessing."

Diana sat on the edge of Sarah's bed, watching as Sarah tried on and rejected one outfit after another. Sarah had walked out of the office the other day, and realized there were only a handful of people she wanted to talk to after such a momentous decision. Caleb Lewis was high on the list—but she hadn't called him.

She wanted him to believe her about that other article, all on his own. Without the knowledge that she had quit the gossip business. Thus far, he hadn't called or come to see her again.

She glanced at the invitation to the party again. Tonight she would see him. But would he be alone? Or would the Caleb Lewis she had written so many articles about be at the bar as he always was, surrounded by women?

God, she was a true glutton for punishment for going to this thing.

"Thanks for coming over, sis," she said to Diana.

Diana waved a hand, as if it was no big deal. "Anytime. And it was high time we started packing up Dad, even if I think moving him is a mistake."

When Diana had arrived at the apartment that Saturday morning, Sarah had reminded her father that today they were packing his things and then moving him over to his other daughter's home tomorrow. Martin Griffin hadn't said much, except that he was going to the store for his favorite coffee and he'd be back.

"What mistake?" Sarah asked, drawing herself back to her sister's statement while she held yet another sweater against her chest and frowned at the reflection in the mirror.

"Moving Dad. He's happy here."

Sarah sighed. "Diana, it's your turn. Quit trying to talk me out of it."

"I'm serious. Did you see him this morning? He looked like he was losing his best friend."

Maybe Diana was right and her father didn't want change any more than Diana did, because as soon as he'd left, she'd checked her cabinet and realized she already had two pounds of her father's favorite blend. Clearly, he hadn't wanted to be here, or to help with the move.

"He'll settle in after a few days and he'll be fine," Sarah said.

Diana let out a long breath, then crossed to the half-packed box in the hallway and picked over a few of the items in it. "Listen, Sarah, I'm not like you. I don't remember to pick up Dad's favorite coffee when I go to the supermarket. I don't have the patience to explain how the remote works. And I sure as hell don't like sitting around at the end of the day rehashing the headlines I already read on the subway that morning."

Sarah bit back her frustration and wondered again if she had done something wrong along the way of helping to raise her sister. "It's called being part of a family, Diana."

"I know. And if Dad wants to go to a baseball game or take a walk or do something... well, interactive, then I'm your girl. But I am not Domestic Diana, not by any stretch of the imagination."

"What better opportunity—"

"If you use that word one more time, I swear, I will hit you with this." She glanced down at the item in her hands. "What is this thing?"

Sarah laughed. "It's the shaving-cream warmer we bought him for Christmas last year. He wanted it because the barber had one and he swears it makes shaving easier."

"See? I don't even remember that conversation.

And I wouldn't even know where to buy one of these..." She looked down at the slim cylindrical steel-and-plastic contraption again. "...warming-up things anyway."

"You'll learn. It's not that hard."

"For you. For me, this is rocket science." Diana sighed. "I just don't think the same way as you do."

Sarah tossed the sweater on her bed, went into her closet, returned with a red blouse and tried again. Ugh. No better. "And what way is that?"

"Like Mom did."

Those words made Sarah pause. "Diana—"

"No, let me say this." Her sister got to her feet and crossed to Sarah. "I love you, Sarah, but you're still acting like Mom, even though you don't have to anymore. And even though you think you stopped a long time ago. You still try to take care of all of us, and I'm sure you will even after Dad lives at my place, telling me how to make his dinner or starch his shirts or whatever."

"I won't. I'm looking forward to the freedom."

Diana snorted. "You've always had that freedom, Sarah. You just didn't realize it. We're grown-ups, Dad and me. We don't need you to do any of these things anymore."

The words stung, like a slap of rejection. Was this how they all looked at her? As some kind of hovering mother hen? "I'm not trying to do that."

"Yes, you are. You just step right in and offer your opinion or bring over a casserole or put a missing button back on a shirt."

"That's not so bad."

Diana laughed. "You call me every single day. And you know what you ask me?"

"How you're doing?"

"If I ate lunch. Or dinner, depending on the time. And then you ask where I'm going that night. Half the time, you tell me not to stay out too late because I have a class or have to work."

"I just worry about you."

Diana put out a hand, as if that sentence alone proved her point. "Don't. I'm fine, Sarah. All grown up and everything. It's you I'm worried about."

"Me? I'm fine."

"Because lately you've been happier than I've ever seen you before, and I worry that you're going to let all that go away."

"I'm not letting anything go."

Diana put a fist on her hip. "What about Caleb Lewis?"

Sarah turned away. "Caleb let me go."

"Over a misunderstanding." Diana reached for her sister, and waited until Sarah's gaze met hers. "All your life, you've put everyone else first. It's time you stopped doing that. If you want Caleb, if you, well, if you love him, then you should go for it. Take a chance. Live the life you've always wanted."

"I'm just going to this party to network and—"

"You can lie to me but don't lie to yourself. Go there and fight for what you want."

Sarah worried her lower lip, considering her sister's words. Diana was right. Sarah wasn't going there just to network. She wanted to walk in that room, see Caleb's eyes widen, see the grin on his face as she approached.

Damn it, despite everything, she wanted him.

"I just want to...shine tonight," Sarah said.

"Okay then," Diana said, her voice soft. "Let's find you something amazing."

Sarah nodded and waved Diana toward her closet. "You're the expert."

Diana grinned, already in her element. In this one area, Diana excelled. She had a natural affinity for clothes, makeup, hair. Even if she was going to the gym, she looked like a cover model. Whereas Sarah...

Well, Sarah didn't. She excelled on paper, not

so much in the beauty department. "Do you want to know why I had those shoes?" she said.

Diana poked her head out of the closet. "Which ones?"

"The red stilettos."

"Oh. The one I threw out the window." Diana cringed. "I'm sorry. Again."

"No, it's fine. Really. I didn't bring them home just for the article research. They were more. They were…a symbol, I guess." She took a deep breath, then took a bigger risk in exposing her vulnerabilities. "Of everything about what I wanted to look like and how I wanted people to see me."

Diana gave her sister a curious look. "What are you talking about?"

"The woman who wears shoes like those doesn't look like me." Sarah ran a hand down the jeans and T-shirt she'd slipped back into after her twentieth outfit option had met with rejection. At this rate, she'd end up going to the party looking just like she always did. Not exactly a way to make a memorable entrance. "She wears sexy dresses, and knows how to do her makeup just so, and has hair that curls perfectly over her shoulders. She's witty with men and walks into a room as though she owns it. She wears all those shoes I buy and never wear."

A few days ago, for one moment, she'd felt

like that woman. She had put the stilettos on, and become someone else. Had it really been the shoes, though? Or had she been ready to be someone else, to finally change her life?

Sarah glanced over at Diana, fully expecting a snarky response.

For a moment, her younger sister studied her. If she'd had sarcasm prepared, she let it go. "But, you *are* like those women. Even if you do just let those gorgeous shoes collect dust."

Sarah laughed. "Uh, no, I don't think so. I work in this industry, Diana. I see these women every day. And I'm as far from looking like one of them as Alaska is from Hawaii."

Diana stepped out of the closet and came to stand beside Sarah. She cupped her older sister's jaw, then turned her gently toward the full-length mirror. "You are so wrong, Sarah. You have just as much pizzazz as they do. Look at you, you…" Her voice trailed off.

Sarah glanced over at Diana. "I what?"

A smile wobbled on Diana's face. Her eyes misted and her gaze held tight to the mirror image. "You…you look just like Mom."

Sarah's heart contracted. The moment lingered in the air, and for a long time, neither sister said anything, just stared at the reflection of the one member of their family they'd never have again. In the mirror, Sarah didn't see herself. Or see

Diana. She saw her mother's eyes, her mother's chocolate-colored hair and the long delicate fingers that had plaited braids, rolled out cookies and smoothed away tears.

Then her gaze drifted over to her younger sister, the one who infuriated her one moment and touched her heart in the next. They were so alike, the two of them, and maybe that was why they fought so much. Too close in age, too close in personality and both fighting for something that had slipped away from them in the middle of the night one cold October day.

"So do you," Sarah whispered, gazing at the younger image of herself, and saw there the reflection of the woman who had blessed them with their hair, their eyes, their smiles. "So do you."

Diana's eyes glistened, and she nodded, mute. Sarah drew her little sister tight in against her, and pressed a kiss to her temple. She inhaled the raspberry-almond scent of Diana's shampoo. It was the same shampoo she had used since high school, one that Sarah had given her for her sixteenth birthday. Somehow, it touched Sarah that this one thing had become Diana's favorite, even still.

Diana leaned into Sarah's embrace, and Sarah tightened the curve of her arm. For a while, it felt like they were two little girls again, growing up too fast because their mother was too sick to parent and their father was too stuck in his grief to notice.

"Diana, you were right," Sarah said softly. "I did act too much like a mother and not enough like a sister. I'm sorry."

"It's okay. There were days when I needed that." Diana smiled. "I don't think I ever said thank you, either. So, thank you for all you did, Sarah. For cooking the dinners, ironing my dresses, making sure I stayed in school. I needed you and you were there."

Tears misted in Sarah's eyes, clogged her throat. She could only nod.

"Well," Diana said, stepping back and swiping at her face, "if you're going to make it to this party on time, then I think we need to stop sobbing like a couple of soap-opera queens and concentrate on finding something in your closet that will bring out your inner supermodel."

"Sounds good, sis." Sarah laughed, and felt a weight slide off her shoulders.

"Yeah, it does." Diana paused, then smiled. "Sis."

A simple word, just a few letters, but the sound of it meant that there was a new direction in their relationship. One that took Sarah out of the role of caretaker and put her right beside

Diana, as siblings. They were going to be okay, she and sister. Just fine.

"I think you have your work cut out for you." Sarah picked up a long-sleeved purple dress she'd tried on before, then dropped it back onto the chair. Why she'd ever found that loud, polyester dress attractive, she didn't know. Lord, one would think the fashion tips in the magazine would have sunk in by osmosis or something.

A pile of back issues of *Smart Fashion* littered the comforter of the bed. Diana dropped down beside them and flipped idly through the first one, then turned the issue toward Sarah. "This would look good on you."

Sarah sighed. "Maybe if I was twenty pounds thinner. Look at how tight that skirt is."

Diana laughed. "Live a little, Sarah. This will look good on you, I guarantee it. And I know you have something similar in your closet."

"How do you know that?"

Diana grinned. "Because I gave it to you last Christmas and you never wore it."

"Oh." Sarah offered her sister an apologetic smile. "Sorry."

Diana disappeared inside the small walk-in closet, then emerged a moment later with a skirt, a blouse and a pair of high heels Sarah had bought months ago and never worn. "Here, try this."

Sarah started to protest again, but Diana just shoved the clothes into her hands. Sarah slipped out of her jeans and T-shirt, then into the leopard-print skirt and sheer black blouse. Before she even finished zipping the skirt, she felt different. Sexier. Sleeker. More in control.

The shoes raised her height another four inches and made her legs look longer and leaner. The blouse's deep V-front gave her a cleavage she hadn't even realized was part of her chest. Still, it seemed like something was missing. "This is a great outfit, but…"

"It doesn't have that wow factor." Diana put a fist on her hips and assessed Sarah. "What you need is a dress that will make people talk."

Sarah laughed. "You've seen my closet, Diana. I don't own anything like that."

"Hello, hello!" Their father's booming voice carried through the apartment. "Are you home, Sarah?"

"In here, Dad."

Their father strode into the room. In his arms, he had a large cardboard box. He set it by the door, then gave his daughters a big grin. "I got big news, girls. I've rented my own place. Move in next week. I think it's about damned time I started taking care of myself." He leaned forward, and gave his eldest daughter a wink. "If you ask me, I think it'll be good for me to be on my own. Teach me some responsibility."

Diana snickered.

"Dad, you can live here—"

"No, it's all decided. I'll sure miss your cooking, but I'm doing the right thing, girls. Letting you all have your lives, and me...well, letting me have mine. Besides, I'm just moving down the street into one of those senior citizens' complexes. I hear there's lots of pretty women there." He winked again.

Sarah saw her father's determination, and the excitement in his features. Unlike before, this time he was looking forward to being out on his own. "Sounds great, Dad. I'm happy for you."

"Me, too." Diana came to stand beside her. "Real happy."

"You're just glad you didn't have to learn how to cook for me," Martin said with a laugh.

Diana chuckled. "That, too."

Martin grabbed the box out of the corner and handed it to Sarah. "Oh, I almost forgot. Somebody left that in your hall. It's heavier than heck. I don't know what it is, but it's a hell of a lot more than flowers."

Sarah laid the box on the bed, then removed the lid. Nestled inside a bed of tissue paper lay a vibrant red dress, a deep, rich crimson, and a pair of matching stilettos with a bow on the heel and another on the strap.

Her shoes. Her design. Right here, in living color. She lifted the dress out of the box, and as she did she saw the label sewn inside. LL Designs.

Caleb.

"That's gorgeous," Diana said. "And those shoes...to die for."

A smile filled Sarah's face as she took in the ruby stilettos, the dress. Everything. "They're not just gorgeous, they're...adventurous. Spirited. Jeweled."

"Jeweled?" Martin said. "What the hell is that supposed to mean? I don't see no rubies on there."

"It means Caleb listened." Sarah clutched the dress to her chest and stood in front of the mirror, admiring the way the satiny fabric hung on her body. She held the shoes against her chest, amazed at how the slight bell bottom of the dress reflected the sweet bows of the shoes, while the deep scalloped neck added a degree of forties'-style sexy that would definitely catch some attention. He'd done this, dare she hope, just for her?

"Caleb, huh?" Her dad grinned. "I knew I liked that boy."

Sarah sent a smile at her father and sister. "So

do I." She ran a hand down the soft fabric. "So do I."

"Well, put it on," Diana said, giving Sarah a little shove toward the closet. "This we have to see."

A few minutes later, Sarah emerged. The dress fit perfectly, and the shoes seemed custom-made for her feet. They slid on with no effort, and curved along her arch, her toes, with a familiarity that made it seem as if she'd owned them all her life.

Her father let out a low whistle. Diana gasped. Sarah stepped in front of the mirror and saw a woman transformed. Not just by what she was wearing, but by everything she had done and gone through in the last days. "Isn't it amazing," Sarah said, "how a simple outfit can make you look and feel like someone else?"

Diana came up behind her and put her hands on Sarah's shoulders. "You always were that woman, sis. She was just waiting inside you for you to let her come out and play with makeup."

Sarah laughed. "Yeah, I think you're right."

"I think this calls for a celebration," Martin said. "I'm getting a beer. You girls want anything?"

Sarah and Diana laughed. "We're good, Dad."

Once Martin left the room, Diana reached up and unclasped the clip holding Sarah's hair in a messy bun, then smoothed her older sister's hair onto her shoulders. "All my life, you've taken care of me, Sarah. And you were great at it, really. But I think you forgot to take care of you."

"Diana—"

"No, I need to say this, Sarah. The other day, when I threw that shoe out the window, I was childish and mean and...wrong. I acted like a two-year-old."

"You..." Sarah stopped. "Okay, maybe you did."

"After that, I went home and stewed and stomped around my apartment, and then I got out this." Diana crossed to her purse and pulled out a thick photo album. Sarah knew without looking what was in it. More than a decade's worth of photos, assembled after their mother got sick, as Sarah tried to fill an album with memories that she wanted to hold on to. Memories that seemed to slip out of her grasp more every day. "Do you remember that time we played dress-up?"

Sarah smiled. "We were always doing that."

"Yeah, but one day we dressed up as each other. You put on one of my pretty little ballet dresses, and a pair of Mom's heels. You even wore the tiara." Diana laughed. "And I—"

"You put on my dark-brown jumpsuit. God, that thing was ugly. Why did I ever go out in public in it?"

Diana laughed. "You used to love that ugly thing."

"Clearly, I had no taste. Even back then."

"Well, I'm not going to argue with that, especially after seeing a picture of that jumpsuit again." Diana's green eyes danced with a tease. "Do you remember how you acted when you wore the ballet skirt?"

A flush filled Sarah's cheeks. "I ran around the house like I was Clara in *The Nutcracker*. Thought I could dance. Unfortunately, I definitely couldn't."

"You were a totally different person. All fun and lightness. And yes, you did dance like a chicken in the living room." Diana laughed. "The point is, when you slipped out of being you for a little while, you had fun."

"I have fun."

"Uh-huh." Diana grabbed an issue of *Smart Fashion,* flipped several pages in the magazine, then turned it toward Sarah. "Now there's a man who turns *exciting* into a verb. Are you having fun with him?"

Caleb Lewis's grin stared back at her. The

light from the camera had caught his blue eyes just right and they seemed to twinkle, to tease. To dare her. Damn, she missed him. She missed him every time he walked away.

Sarah sighed. "That's complicated."

"You want him," Diana said.

"I do not." Sarah shook her head, then glanced again at Caleb's image. A handsome man she'd found impossible to forget. "Okay, maybe a little."

"Then put on the ballet skirt, sis. And show this man you're ready to dance."

CHAPTER TWELVE

THE woman standing across the jam-packed room was not Sarah Griffin. Couldn't be.

Caleb took a step forward, peering through the layer of fog created by fog machines hanging from the ceiling, trying to see past the hundreds of people packing the room, and watched as the woman descended the stairs and entered the nightclub. If he hadn't sent her the dress and shoes himself, he'd never have believed that it was her wearing it because she had truly been transformed.

The silky red fabric skimmed her curves, hitching a little with each step. It grazed against her legs, stopping just above her knees. The scalloped neck dropped into a tantalizing curve across her cleavage. She'd pinned half her hair up onto the top of her head, leaving a cascade of curling tendrils to frame her face, drift along her shoulders, her back. She'd exchanged her glasses for a pair of contacts, which only made her eyes seem bigger, more luminous, particularly when paired with the dark red jewel tone of the dress.

And the shoes…they were amazing. They accentuated her legs and emphasized the definition of her calves. Caleb's gaze traveled down her slender frame, then up, then down again.

Around him, he heard people murmuring about the dress. Calling it a showstopper. A gotta-have-it. He saw several women glancing over at Sarah's shoes, and knew without a doubt he had a winner on his hands. But he didn't care. The public would see the rest of the collection when Fashion Week started tomorrow, and the orders would surely pour in, revitalizing LL Designs.

He made his way through the crowd, ignoring the people who tried to get his attention. He couldn't close the gap between himself and Sarah fast enough. The words he needed to say burned in his throat. He'd been so wrong, and he knew the dress and shoes were barely a beginning of an apology, but he hoped tonight he could make her see that he was sorry. When he reached her, though, his intentions stumbled with his nerves. "I see you got my gift."

"I did. Thank you."

"You look…amazing," Caleb said. "Stunning."

A smile curved across Sarah's face. "Jeweled?"

He laughed. "That, too."

Sarah waved toward the stilettos. "These are amazing. Even better than the Frederick K shoes."

"They're your design."

She smiled. "But you picked the color. And this deep ruby red is just so…vibrant."

"Like you. I couldn't imagine a better color for you, Sarah Griffin." He grinned, then put out a hand to her. "Let's head to somewhere a little quieter. I want to talk to you."

She went to put her hand into his, then drew back. "Before we do, let me ask you something. Do you still think I wrote that article about your mother?"

"That's what I want to talk to you about. But not here. Let's go—"

She shook her head, and everything inside him ached to touch her, but she was already backing away. He reached for her, but she slipped out of his grasp. "I can't do this, Caleb. I'm sorry."

"Sarah!"

Caleb started to follow her into the sea of people that had swallowed her up when he felt someone clap him on the shoulder. He turned back, about to tell whoever it was that he didn't have time to talk. Then stopped.

"So, you ready to sell yet?" Frederick K's voice boomed above the music, the conversations of those around them. "Because my offer is going down every day."

"Stop wasting your breath, Frederick."

"Come on, Caleb. Why are you hanging on to a sinking ship? Hell, the whole world knows that LL Designs is nothing without Lenora."

"The company is fine." Caleb scanned past Frederick K's shoulder, searching for Sarah's form in the crowd.

"Oh, yeah? That's not what I hear the tabloids are going to be saying tomorrow." A vicious grin slid across the burly designer's face. He leaned in toward Caleb, as if he was going to share a secret. "Might want to check *Behind the Scenes.* I think they have a thing or two to say about your chances of success now that the company's namesake is gone."

Caleb's fists clenched at his sides, but he held himself in check. Every part of him wanted to slap that grin right off Frederick K's face. "What, it wasn't enough for you to put the other article in there? Yeah, I know about that. Your friend Karl told me everything when I talked to him yesterday. Admitted you fed him all that information about my mother. I don't know how or why you did that, and I don't even care. It was low and mean."

Frederick K laughed. "Come on, my boy, get real. It's called doing business. I call in a few tips to *Behind the Scenes* and they do what they want with them. Someone had to let the world know Lenora wasn't ever getting behind the wheel of the company again. Look at it this way—I did you a favor. Now you can sell to me and not have to worry about public perception. People will understand. You did your best, now let that albatross go. To me."

"You'll never own so much as a button from this company," Caleb said, advancing on Frederick K and emphasizing his point with a finger in the other man's ample chest. "Now get out of my face before I do something you regret."

"Like what? Try to convince your little reporter friend to write something bad about me?" Frederick K leaned in toward Caleb.

"The media is good for more than just helping your star rise to the top," Caleb said. "They're also great at getting the truth out there. Like the truth about what a horrible human being you are. In fact, I'm not even sure you are a human."

"Oh, you think can threaten me?" Frederick K snorted. "I have the media in my back pocket, my boy, right there with my wallet. Thanks to them, I'm the darling of the fashion world."

"I know one reporter who wouldn't find you

darling at all." Caleb grinned. "And I guarantee this is the perfect story for her to cover. And not for one of those tabloids, either. Oh, no, you and your meteoric, *paid* rise to the top, that's one of those stories that deserves to be front and center in a news magazine."

A shaky laugh escaped Frederick K. "Come on, Caleb. This was all about a little friendly competition. No harm, no foul."

This time, Caleb was the one who grinned. He was going to love seeing this story, the one that exposed Frederick K as a fraud who had manipulated the media into creating his success. "Funny, it didn't feel so friendly to me. And I'm going to make sure everyone knows what kind of person you are."

Frederick K took several steps back, jostling the group of people behind him. "I'll, ah, talk to you later. Maybe we can catch up after Fashion Week?"

"No. We can't."

The other man just pivoted away, blending into the crowd so fast, it was almost like he wasn't there.

Martha came up beside him. "What was that all about?"

"A...life lesson." He put a hand on Martha's arm. "I'll talk to you later. I have something to do right now. Someone I have to find." Caleb scanned the crowd, searching for a crimson dress among all the black and blue and gold that filled the space.

"If you're looking for the person I hope you are, try over there." Martha gestured toward Sarah, who was sitting on a stool at the bar.

Caleb crossed the room in record time, navigating between the groups of people like a NASCAR driver. When he reached Sarah, he smiled at her, but she didn't return the gesture. That didn't bode well, but he was far from ready to give up.

"Do you want to dance?" he asked.

She stirred her drink and shook her head. "Caleb, no one's dancing here."

"There's music. Space out there." He thumbed back toward the center of the room. "I say that's all we need. Besides, I set my own rules, remember?"

She arched a brow and nodded toward the reporters hanging on the periphery of the room. "Are you sure you want to give the tabloids more fodder for their issues?"

He put out a hand and waited for her to put her delicate palm in his. She hesitated, then after what seemed an eternity, slid off the stool and put her hand in his. As soon as they touched, a calmness drifted over Caleb, as if he'd been searching for something for weeks, months, years, and he had finally found it. "I don't care what they write about me. I only care what you write, in your head."

"I'm not writing anymore, at least not for *Behind the Scenes*. I quit."

"Good. You deserve better than that." He led her to the center of the room, then slipped a hand around her waist. She curved against him perfectly, fitting to the planes of his chest as if she'd been made for him. "I owe you an apology, Sarah. I should have trusted you about the article, and I should have listened when you tried to tell me the truth."

"I understand why you would have believed I did it. I mean, my name was right there, in black and white."

"But you were there in Technicolor, and I should have listened to the source, not the tabloid."

She smiled up at him. "I think you're learning the news business, Mr. Lewis."

"As much as you've learned the fashion one. Speaking of which, I have a story for you. One that is guaranteed to get the editor of any *respected* publication—" He put extra emphasis on the word *respected*. "—drooling."

"What is it?"

The bluesy music curled around them, and the rest of the people seemed to drop away. Caleb waltzed Sarah to the right, his hand lying easily against her back. "I'll tell you later. Tonight is just about us."

"And the five hundred other people here?"

He laughed. "Yeah." He spun her in a tight, small circle, and she pressed into him on the turn. Desire raced through his veins, and Caleb leaned down to kiss her, but at the last second, Sarah drew back.

"Caleb, what are we doing?"

"Kissing, I hope."

"I meant with us."

"We're dancing and I'm telling you again that I was wrong," he said. "And you were right."

"Meaning?"

They sashayed back and forth as the music shifted from the bluesy slow song to one with a little bit faster tempo. "I believed what I wanted to believe about that article because it was easier. Easier than dealing with the ramifications of the truth."

"Ramifications?"

"If I admitted to myself that you weren't that evil reporter I've always painted you to be, and that you were the wonderful woman that you are, I would have also had to admit that I was afraid to…" He paused, looked down at her sweet lips, and smiled. "…fall in love with you."

She opened her mouth to respond, then shut

it again. Her eyes widened in shock. He liked that he had surprised her into silence.

"And yes, Sarah, I fell in love with you." He brushed a lock of hair off her face, then let his hand linger along her cheek. Her skin was like satin against his palm. "I think I fell in love with you the first time I talked to you."

"You...you fell in love?"

He nodded and smiled. She returned the smile, and joy took root in his heart. "You are the most amazing woman I've ever met, Sarah. You're strong, and independent and you have a way of bringing out the best in me."

"Just the best?" A grin teased him. "Or the worst, too?"

"Only the best. You expect more out of me," Caleb said. Another couple stepped out onto the floor beside them, apparently with the same idea of dancing, but he ignored them. He was only aware of Sarah, and the intensity of her eyes when they looked at him. "More than I ever thought I could give. You were right, I wasn't happy. I wasn't taking chances. I guess that's because everything always came easy to me. I breezed through college, got the first job I applied for, never had to worry about money. Never faced anything that I couldn't tackle."

"Until you took over LL Designs."

"Yeah. That shook me. I mean, here I was, this

success at everything else I tried and I couldn't make this work. The one thing that mattered. To me, to my mother, to the employees."

"You were a fish out of water, that's all."

"No, I was a fish who wasn't being smart about my job. It wasn't until I looked outside the tank, so to speak, that I found what I needed."

"What was that?"

"You." He grinned. "You gave me not just the insight I needed to change the way I thought about the company's designs, but also exactly the right design for the launch of the shoe line."

"I did all that?" Her face brightened, and he drew her close again as they turned and dipped. She felt so right in his arms that he couldn't imagine ever letting her go.

He nodded. "And more. Maybe you should consider working for me."

"Working for you?" A smile whisked across her features, one that held a tease. "That could get dangerous."

He trailed a finger along her lips. "That's what I was hoping."

"Being together like that, every day, well, some people would call that a relationship. And if I remember right, you were very busy perfecting your bachelor-playboy image."

"Not anymore. I'm done with that life." He let out a sigh, and his tone shifted from playful to serious. "For a long time, I used those places to escape. To forget how I was screwing up the one thing that mattered to my mother. I was caught in this limbo, unable to make the right decision where she was concerned, unable to save the business. How could I possibly think I could handle a relationship?" He swung her around the other couple who had started dancing beside them. Sarah was light in his arms, her steps easily matching his, as if she were reading his mind. "So I dated people that required nothing out of me. And I got the same in return."

"Nothing."

He nodded, then smiled down at her. "Until I met you. You gave me so much, Sarah, not just in the last two weeks, but in the moment when I needed you most. You were there, and it meant so much more than I can tell you. Thank you."

"You're welcome." She leaned against him, her head resting on his chest. He inhaled the light floral scent of her shampoo and knew he would never forget this moment. This dance. "You did the same for me. You forced me to realize that I could talk all I wanted to about living my own life, but until I actually put on the shoes and walked the walk, I wasn't leaving that rut."

"And you do wear those shoes well."

A flush filled her cheeks and she looked up,

shooting him a coy smile. "Why thank you, Mr. Lewis."

"Oh, we're back to that, are we?" He leaned in closer to her. "Well, if that's the case, then I think I'd better remind you of my name." He kissed her, deeply, thoroughly, not caring if the entire room was watching them. From far off, he heard the click of cameras. Didn't matter. Nothing was keeping him from this woman, not anymore.

When he drew back, she exhaled a long breath. Desire shimmered in her eyes, and beneath his palm, he felt her pulse race. "Wow. That was amazing, Caleb."

He grinned. "See? I knew I'd be able to refresh your memory."

"Oh, you did, and you did a lot more than that."

"Like what?"

Her smile returned, and reached into her eyes. "You aren't the only one who fell in love."

Joy burst in his heart like fireworks. Had she really said that? He felt like a teenager again, with the same rush of a first love. Maybe, after all, Sarah *was* his first true love. Because he couldn't remember ever feeling this way about anyone else. "You love me?"

She nodded, the smile he knew as well as his own filling her face. "I do."

"Oh, God, Sarah, I love you, too." He drew her against him and stopped dancing. Instead, just holding her. Long and tight. Drawing in the scent of her, the feel of her body against his, wanting to preserve this moment forever. "And I don't want to spend another day without you. Marry me, Sarah."

She drew back, her eyes wide. "Marry you? But...but we barely know each other."

"True. We have worked together a lot over the last couple of weeks, but this *is* our first official date, after all."

"And we should date a lot before we do something like get engaged."

"We should." He grinned. "So, what are you doing in an hour?"

She laughed. "Nothing."

"Great. Then let's go on our second date in an hour. And another hour later, our third. And keep going like that until we end up in a church." He tipped her chin until her mouth was just below his. Heat filled the space between them, and desire coiled tight in his gut. "Because I am never letting you go, Sarah Griffin. You are the best thing that has ever happened to me and all I want to do is marry you."

"That's crazy. It's—"

"A total step out of our comfort zones." He waved down at the floor, at his shiny dress shoes

and her brand-new, designed-entirely-by-her stilettos. "At least we're wearing the right shoes for
doing that."

She laughed, then pressed herself against him.
She curved into his arms as if she had been
made for just that spot, and held him tight. "Oh,
Caleb, we don't need the shoes at all," she said
softly, "we just need each other."